Everything She Never Imagined

Kaydeen A. Hutchinson

Everything **She Never Imagined**

This book is a work of fiction. Names, characters, places, and incidents either are products of the author's imagination or are used fictitiously. Any resemblance to actual events or locales or persons, living or dead, is entirely coincidental.

Manufactured and published in the United States of America

ISBN-13: 978-0692596531

ISBN- 10: 0692596534

ALSO BY KAYDEEN A. HUTCHINSON

Nothing **She Ever Had (part 1)**

DEDICATION

To all my supporters, family & friends, this one is for you.

« CHAPTER 1 »

"OKAY, AND HERE you are," said the bartender as she placed two large frozen margaritas in front of Karen and I before continuing.

"Are you ladies closing out or running a tab?"

"We're going to go ahead and run a tab; here you go," I replied as I handed her my credit card.

"Not a problem, I'll get you guys all set up," she responded cheerfully with a smile.

"Oh, yes, just what I needed for this summer heat," said Karen as she sipped her drink before leaving the bar.

"Yes, this was definitely needed, especially with the heat and humidity," I replied as I carefully picked up my drink making certain not to spill it.

Heading back to the cabana, we tried desperately to walk as fast as possible to avoid any extra rays. With it being the beginning of the summer, I decided to take some time off from work to just relax and catch up. Even though I enjoyed my job and the people that I worked with, I was way overdue for my *me* time.

South Beach always afforded me the opportunity to let go and just live. There was never a moment when I came here that I didn't find something or someone to entertain me. People from all walks of life were known to venture here, just to have that South Beach experience. Strangely enough, even as a local, I was still somehow intrigued by its inherent madness.

Not to mention that it had been a while since I've been to any hot spots in south Miami. Since the incident with Lawrence and Charles, I've kind of been off the radar, so to speak. I was simply working and trying to advance in my career. Not doing too much and definitely not dating. I just couldn't see myself being a happy and content person if my priorities weren't in line and my goals outlined. There was no way in hell I was going to get caught up in another *relationship* and not come out on top. At this point whoever comes into my life has got to be ready to star in the *Leah Show*. Simply put, I'm a bitch on a mission and I'm taking no prisoners.

But don't misconstrue things; like any other chick I definitely had my pieces on the side. I just wasn't ready to make anyone or anything official. I keep a friend or two for my own personal gratification, but no one, and I mean no one, has yet to make it past the *friend* stage. And for now, that's exactly how I intend on keeping it.

On a more positive note, things have actually been going great for me. My career choice compliments my work ethics and overall career goals, the money is equally complimentary, and the opportunity for advancement is far beyond what I had originally imagined. Last Tuesday was my third year anniversary with Merlich & Co, and if all goes as planned, I'll soon become one of the youngest top officials throughout the entire firm.

As far as Charles is concerned, it appears that he is up to his same conniving ways. Just the other day, Karen and I caught a news update on how he took detectives on a wild goose chase in an attempt to uncover money that he had apparently hidden during his laundering reign. From what I hear, he made a deal with police that if he helped them recover the money, they would turn over a portion of the funds which he actually worked for into accounts for his children. Reluctantly, and for unknown reasons, the police agreed and took him out of his cell for a couple of days to help them search and uncover the funds. Turns out it was all a hoax and the police ended up finding nothing.

Honestly, I wasn't surprised; being the deceitful person that he is known to be, I was certain that it was nothing more than a failed attempt to garner extra attention.

Shortly after being sentenced, Charles tried desperately to make contact with me. He's written emails and wrote letters pleading with me to at least respond so that he can clear his good name. In one particular email, he insisted that it was all Lawrence's idea and that he never intended to hurt me. Knowing that it was all a bunch of bull, I decided to not even respond and afford him the opportunity to interfere and disrupt my healing phase. I wanted nothing else to do with Charles; ever.

Similar to Charles, Lawrence also refuses to let go. Every chance he gets he makes it a point to profess his undying love for me. It's been three years and I still get random texts, emails, and phone calls. And just like his co-conspirator, he too claims that it was all Charles's idea to include me in the "pack." According to Lawrence, Charles showered him with gifts and money for him to simply stay acquainted and go along with his eccentric plans.

Regardless of who's telling the truth, I want nothing to do with either of them. I've known Lawrence for far too long, and if it hadn't been Charles, it would have been someone else. There were countless times during the course of our relationship that I either caught him with someone or was told that he was seeing someone else. It was just a matter of time before everything came crashing to an end.

Although initially unfortunate, my past experiences have undoubtedly made me the woman I am today. I am keener to lies, games, and just overall foolery. Charles taught me a very valuable lesson and that is to trust no man. Some may say I'm a woman scorned, but I say I'm a woman of experience.

As they say, fool me once shame on you, fool me twice shame on me.

"Leah, I know I have said this to you before, but I am so very proud of you. If no one else has told you, I can truly say that I have witnessed you overcome and grow as a person. Hell, I tell people all the time that I have friends in high places, so don't mess with me," said Karen.

A smile quickly spread widely over my face. "Awe, thanks boo," I replied gleefully and continued, "I know if no one knows, you surely do. And thanks for having my back through it all, I couldn't ask for a better friend."

"You know I wouldn't have it any other way," replied Karen, blushing slightly.

As we sat under the cabana, we drank, ate, and talked until it was almost sundown. Being that Karen was in a new and proclaimed serious relationship, we didn't get to see much of each other; at least not the way that we used to. So it was pertinent that I brought her up to speed with what was really going on. We talked about the job, Lawrence, Charles, and her new, yet mysterious man.

"I think I maybe a little tipsy," I replied blissfully.

"Here we go again; we can't have two drinks without you getting drunk," added Karen.

"A lady never gets drunk, it's more like tipsy," I replied in a theatrical kind of way.

"Hmm, well I'm feeling a little nice myself. Ms. Cheery definitely made these drinks; she may just be as good as me. Oh, but listen," Karen interjected excitedly. "I know what we can do. Let's go check out that new karaoke spot off Biscayne."

"What new spot?" I asked.

"Oh, God, do I have to keep you updated on everything? I don't even go out like I used to and I can still tell you what's hot in these streets. It's the newest spot that everyone is talking about. I think it's called La Mere, they do karaoke there on Wednesday and other things throughout the week. From what I hear it's a really nice vibe."

"Well, then what are we waiting on? Let's do it!"

∞∞∞

From the moment we pulled up to the building, it was evident that this was in fact the new hot spot. The parking lot was jammed packed and cars outlined the outside curb.

Thankfully Karen and I decided to hold off on getting there and made time to refresh. With Karen now living in south Broward and not wanting to make the drive home, I decided to have her shower and change at my place. There was no way that we would be entering any establishment, especially in Miami, without looking our absolute best. It was simply a diva code violation that I couldn't fathom breaking.

"Let's hurry up and go in. The way this parking lot is looking, if we don't hurry we probably won't be able to find any seats," added Karen as she flipped up the interior visor mirror.

"That's exactly what I was thinking, and I'm definitely not trying to stand around all night," I quickly replied.

In less than five minutes we were out of the car and walking up to the entrance. "Well, hello ladies," said the buffed bouncer at the door.

"Hello," we replied simultaneously.

"Do you lovely ladies have IDs?"

After showing him our IDs, we proceeded to walk inside. As I was walking in I felt a sudden tug on my right arm.

Quickly turning around, I realized that it was the bouncer trying to garner my attention.

"Sorry if scared you, but I must say that you are a very gorgeous woman. What's your name, beautiful?"

"Lilah," I replied, lying through my teeth.

"Oh, Li-lah," he repeated slowly. "Well, Lilah, I would really love if I could see you again."

"Yeah, that would have been nice, but I'm in a serious relationship at the moment. Sorry."

"Lucky man," he replied with his eyebrows slightly raised.

"One would assume."

After giving off a flirtatious, yet annoying smile, he continued, "Enjoy your night, beautiful."

Stepping inside, I gazed around the room to see if I could spot Karen. Almost immediately, I spotted a hand waving freely in the air; peering closely I realized it was Karen.

As I began walking towards her, it felt like all eyes were conveniently placed on me. Although the building looked fairly large on the outside, the inside was quite the opposite. Though nice, it was extremely small and undeniably congested. All of the tables appeared to be touching and the stage seemed like a small area that was sectioned off just for the night.

"How did you get a seat so quickly?" I asked Karen curiously.

"Like really quickly!" she replied. "Luckily as soon as I walked in, there was a couple that looked like they were getting ready to leave. So me being me, I politely slipped right into their spot the minute they rose from their chairs. And the minute I sat down, the people in front of me started looking crazy, like they pre-selected the seats or something. I was waiting on one of them to say something out of the way, without a doubt it would have been some problems in here tonight; I promise you."

"Oh, God, not tonight, Karen. Let's just have a drama free, fun filled night; the place is already congested."

"I'm just thinking ahead, you know how some people can get."

"Alright, Ma, we're good now. So what are we drinking?" I added in an attempt to change the subject and relax the mood. "And I'm kind of hungry, actually," I continued.

"Yeah, I am as well. Where in the hell are the waitresses? My God, I've been sitting here for over ten minutes."

As soon as Karen finished her last word, a waiter approached our table.

"Hello, ladies, my name is Walter and I'll be taking care of you tonight. Can I start you off with some drinks?" yelled the waiter loudly in an attempt to speak over the awful singing.

"Umm, I'll take an apple martini, please," I replied.

After making our food and drink orders, we continued to sit at the table as we quietly observed the rowdy mixed crowd. Gazing around the room, I noticed a familiar face. Squinting in the same direction, I peered through the crowded room, picking my brain on how I knew this person.

As I continued to look on, it became apparent that the mysterious person seemed to notice me as well, as they quickly turned in my direction and began to smile.

And then all of a sudden it hit me; to my dismay the person smiling back was actually Jasmine; the red head from the lifestyle party. Returning the smile, I swiftly waved my hand as a friendly acknowledgement. Immediately after seeing this, she leaped from her seat and made her way to our table.

"Hey, boo!" blurted Jasmine.

"Hey, mama!" I replied as I stood up to give her a hug.

"How have you been? It's been such a long time," I added.

"Oh my God, I know! It's so great to see you, though. But I've been good; you know, doing my thing and trying to make it work," she replied.

"That's awesome; good to hear. But where are my manners? Jasmine this is Karen and Karen, this is Jasmine."

"Hello," said Jasmine as she extended her hand out for a shake.

"Nice to meet you," replied Karen, not seeming too interested in the greeting.

"So, how have you been doing?" asked Jasmine.

"I've been wonderful; hanging in there," I replied.

"I hear that, I thought I would never see you again. I tried finding you on Facebook, Twitter, you name it; but there were so many Leah's that showed up and for the life of me I couldn't remember your last name." said Jasmine.

After a brief and awkward silence she continued.

So I'm dying to ask, has your boy tried to contact you yet?"

"Who? Charles? He's been calling and writing since the moment he got locked up," I replied.

Shaking her head in apparent disbelief, she continued, "He has been calling and writing me nonstop as well! And the crazy part is, I told him long before the incident happened that I want nothing else to do with him; I'm tired of the lies and the games."

Confused, I knitted up my brows as I waited for her to continue.

"I'm not sure if you know this or not, but Charles and I were dating off and on for the past five years. When I saw him with you at the party the first night, we were technically 'off,' but it was still just so disrespectful to me. So after I confronted him about it, he got, like, really angry and demanded that I go outside and introduce myself to you; or in his words 'I would truly be sorry.' At the time I was confused, hurt, and fearful of what he would do if I didn't follow his orders. So I played nice; I'm sure you know that Charles can be a very domineering man. He just has a way of getting you to do the things he wants you to do. It was like I was under some sort of trance."

Shocked, I became speechless. Never in a million years would I have imagined Charles actually dating Jasmine. I mean, she just didn't seem like his type; if he even had a type. Lately it seems like the more time that goes by, the more I find out. Charles was nothing short of a monster. He had us all wrapped up in his whirlwind; like a puppet master pulling all the strings.

"Why didn't you say something, give me a nudge, a clue or something? I mean, I know we didn't know each other quite that well, but maybe, just maybe, this could have turned out differently; together, we probably could have stopped him," I said.

"I know, Leah, but I can't lie, at the time Charles was paying my rent and really all of my bills. I needed the money; it was fast, easy, and effortless. All that was expected of me was to do as I was told and the money would basically keep coming. And to be quite honest, I was in a place where I would do anything that would keep me from going back to the strip club," replied Jasmine.

That explains it, I thought to myself.

 "Listen, we are going to have to talk, because this is just getting crazier and crazier," I finally replied.

After exchanging numbers, we sat at the table and continued chatting.

"Leah, I must say it was nice seeing you again, but before I go I really want to invite you to a party that the group is having this weekend," added Jasmine.

"The group?" I asked.

"Yes, the same group that was hosting the party the night that I met you," she replied.

"Well I'm not really into...."

She cut me off. "Come on, Leah, we have a lot of catching up to do. Besides, it's not like it's strange behavior to you, you've attended numerous parties with Charles."

"I really just want you to come with me, please say yes," she continued.

Taken back, yet intrigued, I contemplated on whether I should take her up on her offer. The way she behaved was if we were best friends in a past life or something, as if we had some kind of weird inherent connection.

While I was initially closed minded to the lifestyle, having attended an array of parties gave me the unprecedented feeling of belongingness. Everyone there was always friendly and welcoming; almost like family.

"Why not," I finally replied.

"Yay!" added Jasmine as she smiled excitedly. "I'll be sure to call you with the details tomorrow; I'm so happy that I ran into you," she continued.

"Sure thing," I replied as I pondered on whether I was making the right decision.

« CHAPTER 2 »

AFTER THE RUN-IN WITH Jasmine, she's been blowing up my phone like we were long lost friends that were recently reunited. In just a few short days she has told me more about herself than I have known about friends I have had my entire life. It's weird to say the least; it's as if she has been longing for someone to just be a listening ear.

Since the incident three years ago, I have been very hesitant and selective in whom I trust. Her wanting to be so close to me in such a short amount of time definitely sends off red flags. I may be open to hanging with her and talking over the phone, but I would definitely be keeping my ears open and my eyes pried. If she had something up her sleeve or harbored any ill intentions for whatever reason, she'll be cut off quicker than she can mentally process what actually happened; no warning, no nothing.

Through conversation and her constant chatter, she managed to slip in the date and time of the group party. Apparently this meeting would take place over the weekend at Virgen nightclub. You see Virgen is one of those places that is not commonly known, or should I say, widely discussed. Having heard about it through conversation with Charles, I'm a little more familiar with what actually takes place there. So when she mentioned that the party would be held at Virgen, I was a little more apt to going.

Being that it was still early in the day and I didn't have to meet up with Jasmine until later that night, I decided to run my usual errands instead of wasting precious weekend time. I managed to complete my grocery shopping, hair appointment, and postal run in record time. Now all that was left was to make it back home in time to meet the cleaning lady, Marisol.

With all the demands in life there was no way in hell that I could ever find time for cleaning; hell, I barely had time to even piece together my thoughts these days. Besides, Marisol was a seasoned G in the cleaning game. She would enter your house with a three-man crew and within 30 minutes flat you would think you would have moved into an entirely different place. Everything was spotless, scrubbed down, and cleaned to perfection.

However, word in Miami is that her business is actually an undercover prostitution ring. From what I hear, it's no secret that depending on the client, she and her "workers" were known for showing up in lingerie and cleaning wands. Clients had the option of ordering a variety of packages, including simple cleaning services, cleaning services with an added massage, and God only knows what else.

But I'm not the one to knock another chick's hustle, if it's what working then work it. It's not a newly discovered secret that sex sells. Point blank. Period. Always has and always will.

After a long and productive day, it was finally time for me to head out and see what all the fuss was about. I got dressed while slowly pampering myself and preparing for what I thought I would never be faced with again: a lifestyle party. Within no time I hopped inside of my all white CLS 550 and was out of the parking lot.

It felt great riding down the roads in something new. Not sure if it's just imbedded in my genes or what, but I tend to get bored easily when I'm forced to do the same thing over and over; like ride the same car or wear the same clothes too many times.

Being a young chick making her own cash, it's imperative that I make the best out of the cards that I was dealt. I sleep great at night knowing that my overall well-being and life's mission is not dependent on a man. If I learned nothing else from Charles, it is to grind hard, stay on point, and watch out for snakes.

As I slowed to get onto the freeway, I put Jasmine's address into the navigational system before turning on my music playlist. Being that the address she gave me was not too far away, I knew that I would be there in no time.

Minutes later, I heard the navigation tell me to make a slight right turn and I would be two tenths of a mile from my destination. I pulled my car up to a guard gate in a well-known affluent neighborhood just outside Coconut Grove.

Did I have the wrong address? Is this the right place? *This couldn't be where Jasmine lived*, I thought to myself.

I mean, I'm not one to be judgmental, but Jasmine sure didn't appear to have it together enough to even slightly be able to afford a home like the ones in this neighborhood. Puzzled, yet curious, I proceed to the gate.

"Umm, 1329 Lancer Drive," I said to the security guard as I read her address off of the dashboard's interior screen.

"Okay, I just need your license, please," replied the guard.

He was tall, light-skinned, extremely slender, and young; couldn't be more than 23 if you asked me.

After recording my information and tag number, he walked back up to my window as he handed me my license. "Have a nice night, beautiful."

"Thank you," I replied, smiling slightly as I gripped the steering wheel, indicating my readiness.

With a plastered smile on his face, he appeared to choke on whatever line he had planned on using next. Edging quietly away from the car he reverted back to the guard hut before reaching his hand inside.

Once inside the development, I was even more impressed. Not necessarily at the size and look of the houses, but more so that Jasmine actually lived in one. She seemed so subtle and not really interested in the nicer things of life. Continuing down the main entrance, I was directed by the navigation to make a right and my destination would be on the left. As I pulled up in the driveway, I immediately called Jasmine to let her know that I had made it.

The house itself appeared to be two stories with a triple garage and a huge front lawn. If this was in fact her place I would definitely have to hand it to her, because this without a doubt was definitely a boss move.

"Hey, boo!" said Jasmine excitedly as she entered the car.

"Hey, mama, you look nice tonight," I replied.

"Aw, thanks," she replied, smiling as she sat down and fastened her seatbelt.

"Nice place, I didn't even know these were back here."

"Yeah, thanks, but it's my dad's place. I just recently moved in with him until I can get some things together," she replied, confirming my previous notions.

"Oh, okay, well it's nice nonetheless," I replied before continuing. "But listen, I know that I attended a couple parties with Charles in the past, but I'm still a little hesitant about what actually goes on."

"Oh, don't worry, you'll be fine. It's at a public place this time with lots of outside people, so you really don't have anything to worry about. I mean, the way the club is set up you can either stay on the dancing side that's like a regular club or you can go to the private side where the action is actually happening."

"That's different. Driving by I would have never thought that it was actually that kind of spot," I replied.

"I know it's not one of those clubs that is promoted or widely talked about. I must say that it's different and can get wild at times, but you'll be fine," she replied.

Looking at her with a side eye and a little uncertainty, I decided to say nothing further. True enough, no one put a gun to my head and forced me to come out, but I wanted to be certain that it would all be worth it. After all, the adventurous side of me was begging for a little action as long as I wasn't the starring role.

There was just no way I could sanely continue on with such an unbalanced work/social life. It was time for me to take back what was mine, and what better way to kick things off then with some pure unadulterated fun?

"Okay, so we're here, and I think valet is open tonight. Just pull up to the entrance right there," said Jasmine as she pointed near the right side of the club.

Soon after parking we made our way to the door where were immediately greeted by the guy standing there.

"IDs please," he said assertively.

"We're here for the group meeting in the back," added Jasmine as she rummaged through her purse.

 "Okay, right this way ladies," he said after checking our IDs.

From the moment I walked in, nothing really seemed out of the ordinary; in fact everything seemed too normal. The dance floor was small with circular tables situated in an orchestrated arrangement. Two bars sat on each side of the room and a handful of patrons huddled around as they mingled.

Continuing on, it appeared as if he was leading us towards a dark rectangular doorway near the rear of the building. Passing through the doorway brought us to a long dark corridor that appeared seemingly endless. As we walked through the hallway, I could still hear the music blasting on the other side of the wall, the sound of the bass pulsated the building. Still calm, I eagerly anticipated what the other side would bring. It was if time stood still and everything began happening in slow motion. With the people in front of me barely visible, I wasn't sure if I was walking fast or slow or if we were even close to where we were going. Then almost in an instant, a big flash of light illuminated the hallway as an adjacent door flew open.

"Okay, here we are; just check in with that guy over there and he'll take care of you from here," said the door guy.

"Thanks," we both replied.

As I made my way over to the host, I did a quick yet subtle scan of the room. Contrary to the few house parties that I have attended, there appeared to be no rules in this type of setting. People were all over the place drinking, eating, and socializing like it was happy hour at a bar. Many were blatantly naked, a few had on bathing suits, and only handfuls were completely dressed. Once we checked in with the hostess we made our way over to the bar.

"I'll take one of the strongest drinks you make," I said to the bartender with a look of utter seriousness.

After snickering briefly, she turned towards Jasmine. "And for you?"

"I'll do a vodka and tonic with a twist of lime, please."

"You got it," replied the bartender before turning away.

"So, what do you think so far?" Jasmine asked.

Turning to her with a mimicking smile, I hesitated before replying. "Well, it's nothing I haven't witnessed before, I just have to adapt to the fact that things are more in a public setting."

"Yeah, well at least you knew exactly what to expect this time, and I didn't just bring you out blindly like your boy."

We both laughed simultaneously.

"Oh, God no. Let's just enjoy the night without bringing up Charles; the mention of his name alone still makes me quiver. But to be quite honest with you I'm actually enthralled about it. I can't help but admire the fact that the people that actually attend these parties are just so open, free, and welcoming," I said.

"Very," replied Jasmine while shaking her head in agreement and then continued, "And you know that's what actually drew me into the lifestyle. Every time that I attended a party, everyone was so friendly and kind; almost like family. And sadly for the most of us, that's kind of rare."

"Tell me about it. I'm extra cautious these days with who I interact with, let alone date," I replied.

"Drinks up," yelled the bartender loudly as if to over-talk the music.

After taking our drinks we decided to leave the bar and venture around. To my surprise, after just a couple sips, my body began to feel relaxed and at ease. As we made our way through the club, several people nodded and waved as they continued looking on, perceivably trying to make their stares less obvious. Looking from a distance I noticed that there were several oddly placed doors outlining the left side of the wall.

"What's with the million and one doors?" I asked sarcastically.

"Private rooms. If you click with someone and there's an open room, the two of you, or three of you, can go inside for a more intimate session."

"Wonderful," I replied.

"That it is," replied Jasmine, picking up on my continued sarcasm before continuing. "But it's kind of crowded in here, let's go out back and check out the pool area."

As we began making our way closer to the back, we were stopped dead in our tracks by an unknown male.

"Hey, stranger," said the guy as he stood directly in front of Jasmine.

"Steven! What's been going on? Long time no see, man," replied Jasmine excitedly with a rambunctious lingering smile.

"I know, I know. Just been working and trying to get things right," he replied.

Immediately after finishing his last sentence, he diverted his attention towards me.

"Hello, I'm Steven, a long time friend of Jasmine and her family; nice to meet you," said the guy as he extended his hand for a shake.

"Nice to meet you, Steven," I replied, shaking his hand.

Firm grip, I thought inwardly.

Without having to pay too much attention, Steven's sex appeal and features were undeniable. He was tall with smooth, dark brown skin that seemed to never have experienced as much as a breakout. His cheekbones were prominent with eyes that seemed to tantalize. With a dark and thick perfectly lined goatee, he would put anyone in the mind of Morris Chestnut during his most primitive years.

"Are you new to the group?" asked Steven.

"Well, I'm not in any particular group, just came to check out the scene, really," I replied.

"Okay, nice. I'm surprised I never met you before, how long have you guys been friends?"

"A while," interjected Jasmine before I even had a chance to respond.

"Well, any friend of Jasmine is a friend of mine; welcome," he replied.

"Thank you. Again, it was nice meeting you," I replied smiling, attempting to cue Jasmine that I was ready to end the awkward encounter.

As we said our good-byes, we slowly began our walk back towards the outside. It was obvious that Steven wanted to say more, but as luck would have it, someone called out his name before he could counteract our informal gestures. Even though I was opening myself up for dating, I wanted nothing to do with any guy that was overly attractive; that was nothing more than problems, problems that I had no plans on dealing with.

Without realizing it, I inherently had a thing for buff bodies and a charming smile. Thinking back through time, most of my boyfriends or men that I even considered dating, were men that attracted robust amounts of attention. And with each one of those so-called men, I was cheated on, lied to, and left heartbroken.

So without question it was definitely time to change the stakes. I needed a man that was not very attractive, if at all, and wouldn't be so appealing to other women; or in some cases other men.

However, finances were still at the top of the list. I would make it no secret that my leading man would have to have a certain level of financial security if he even wanted to garner my attention. The perfect man for me would be someone that is not an attention grabber, lives a somewhat low-key lifestyle, but doesn't mind lavishing his blessings freely upon me.

"Hmm, it's actually nice out here," I said aloud as we stepped outside.

"It really is. Let's go sit over by the tables and scope out the scene for a minute," added Jasmine.

As we made our way to a set of lounge chairs outlining the pool, I continued looking around as I admired the scene. The outside area was much larger in size than the club. The actual swimming pool itself was also large, with two adjacent hot tubs in the distance. A row of lounge chairs outlined the immediate area and a small tiki hut sat conveniently off to the side.

A handful of people splashed around in the pool, while a few others lounged in the hot tub as they engaged in conversation and laughter. Bottles of what appeared to be champagne outlined the area, as the sounds of music and laughter pinged through the nights' air.

"Hey. Check out those two," whispered Jasmine eagerly as she gazed towards the tiki hut.

Looking in the same direction, I could clearly see the shadows of a man and a woman getting it on like seasoned jackrabbits. The woman hands appeared to be on the ground as her butt was raised in the air. Standing beside her was a male figure erratically jerking back and forth.

"He must not have gotten any in months," I finally replied.

As we continued to talk, drink, and laugh, we began noticing that the outside area was slowly thinning out. As more and more people trickled out of the pool, one woman in particular found it necessary to start a strip show. Engulfed in her amateur strip routine, she swayed back and forth as she slowly removed her bikini, piece by piece. Finally in the nude, she threw her bikini top into the pool, causing it to land squarely on her partner's head. Shortly after the two exchanged kisses, she stood back up and began twirling around with her index finger pointed to the middle of her head like something of a ballerina.

I can't watch anymore of this, let's go back inside," I replied as I laughed discreetly.

As we stood up to leave, I felt Jasmine's grip on my hand.

"Okay, there's one more spot I wanted to show you before we go back to the club area."

Nodding in agreement, I followed closely behind, curious as to what was next.

Making our way back inside the building, Jasmine proceeded to lead me up a dark flight of stairs that was not in plain sight. It rest conveniently alongside the back wall and could easily be mistaken for a storage area.

After making it up the long flight of stairs, we entered a large dark room with strange looking black cords that hung aimlessly from the ceiling. Silver metal circles and small black leather straps seemed to be attached to each dangling cord. Looking to the right of me, I was greeted with much of the same. The only apparent difference was thick rubber looking cords that extended from the wall. Alongside the cords were wooden rectangular boards with similar looking straps nailed to them. Sitting squarely in the center of the room was a large, gothic looking trunk, which in hindsight seemed out of place, but nonetheless, blended.

"Where are we?" I finally managed to ask.

"This is what everyone likes to call the black room," replied Jasmine, holding her hands up in the air before continuing, "And these are what are known as sex swings. Over there is the BDSM section, and the doors alongside the back are just private rooms that you can rent out."

In awe, I stood quietly before responding. "You know, I have always wanted to physically see one of these places. I've always heard stories and saw a couple pornos, but never really got to visit it firsthand."

"Yeah, some people come here specifically for this room and others just venture up here to watch, adding to the excitement."

"I'm pretty sure they were amused."

"Amusing it is, especially when it's a busy night," added Jasmine as she walked over towards one of the swings.

"Leah, come here for a minute; let me school you on a few things," she continued jokingly.

Chuckling slightly, I began walking towards her.

"So, this is how it works; I see someone has experience!" I blurted out as I watched Jasmine adjust herself in the swing.

"Not really, just saw it done a couple times, that's all. Can you come closer and help me adjust this stupid thing?" she asked.

Holding onto the edge of the swing, I waited for her to position herself comfortably before letting go. And then suddenly without notice, she grabbed a hold of my chin as she forcibly tried to push her tongue in my mouth. Now tightly clasping her hands on both cheeks, I struggled to break free of her tight, ironclad grasp. Grabbing both of her wrists, I pushed backwards with as much force as I could muster. With strength like Goliath, she continued kissing me as she pulled my face closer and closer.

"Please don't resist, you know this is something that you and I both want; let's not continue to be shy about it, let's embrace this shit, Leah," she mumbled, maintaining her iron tight grip.

Struggling to break free, I began fishing around for her lower lip as I plotted how I could sink my teeth into it. Missing her lips, I landed on her tongue as I began biting it with every inch of energy that I had left in my body. Swiftly pulling backwards in apparent disbelief, she shrieked in pain as she stared wildly into my eyes. Dropping to the floor and covering her mouth, her muffled howls echoed throughout the room.

Unsure exactly what to do next, I continued looking on as she slowly began raising her head upwards. Knowing that an attack could possibly be next, I took a couple steps backwards as I mentally and physically prepared for what was to come.

« CHAPTER 3 »

"WHY IN THE HELL WOULD you do that?" asked Jasmine as she clasped her hands over her mouth before continuing. "I thought we shared a bond, Leah. I mean, it's not like we haven't been there before."

"Are you serious? That was a onetime event! I was dating a man that I decide to explore with; that night is not a reflection of my sexual preferences."

"Leah, I just couldn't continue to hide this anymore, I secretly have a thing for you. It's just something about you that I connect with. I have never in my life felt this way about another woman, please tell me you feel the same way, Leah, please," she begged.

Looking on in disbelief, I stared at her as if she had ten heads. "Listen, I'm sorry if I led you on somehow, but as I said, it was just something that I did; nothing more, nothing less."

"I'm sorry if I offended you, I just thought we shared something special that night. It seemed like the feelings were there, but you were just too shy to act on them," replied Jasmine with a look of sympathy.

"I can't do this right now." I added.

As I headed towards the door, I wanted more than anything to just run out of there. What in the hell would give her the idea that I have an unspoken love connection with her?

She is going to find out really quickly that I may be about a lot of things, but falling in love with a chick, especially a broke one, was simply not one of them.

∞∞∞

My weeklong hangouts are definitely starting to take their toll. My body feels drained, like I haven't gotten rest in months. Here it is Sunday morning and I was already pooped like it was the end of the work week.

After the crazy encounter with Jasmine, I decided to spend most of Saturday catching up with family and a few friends. With it being summer, as well as the weekend of a popular annual beach event, a lot of people were in town visiting and hanging out. I must admit that it was extremely refreshing to catch up with a few peeps that I hadn't seen in a while.

Deciding that I would finish up the weekend with a little therapeutic shopping, I rose out of bed earlier than I would have. Being busy at the office, along with barely being social, was starting to make my closet look a little out of whack and outdated. It was time I got my mojo back so that I could re-enter this rat race fashionably. It was no secret here in Miami that if you wanted a good man, you had to be in shape, with a certain level of interpersonal intellect, and be just overall presentable.

Making my way to the kitchen, I decided on a quick breakfast that entailed scrambled eggs, toast, and two small pieces of bacon. After eating, I made a couple phone calls before finally getting dressed and heading out.

While cruising down 595 and bumping my new Rihanna album, I was interrupted by the ringing of my phone. Annoyed, I immediately glanced at the interior screen, only to see that it was Jasmine. Briefly contemplating on whether or not I should answer, I reluctantly went ahead and pressed the talk button.

"Hel-lo," I answered, purposely displaying my annoyance.

"Hey, Leah, what's going on with you?" she asked nonchalantly as if everything were back to normal.

"Just heading out to grab a few things from the mall. What's up?"

"Okay, cool. I was just checking on you and also wanted to apologize again for what happened the other night."

"Look, Jasmine, it happened and I'm over it; no hard feelings, we're still cool," I replied.

"Yeah, but I still feel horrible; I hate that it had to happen the way it did. I just want to somehow…."

I cut her off. "Jasmine it is fine, don't worry about it. And I've got to make a phone call before it slips my mind, so I'll give you a call back a little later."

"Wait, Leah, there's another reason why I called. The guy Steven that we ran into at the club keeps calling and bugging me to give you his number. He keeps going on and on about how he wants to get to know you."

Stopping briefly before responding, I contemplated on her possible motives. After everything that happened, I'm not sure if I can trust anything Jasmine has to say at this point. Was she trying to organize some kind of group meeting? I mean, he did mention the fact that they are long time friends. Was this some kind of well thought out plan to get me, her, and another guy into bed?

"Steven? Isn't that your friend?" I finally replied.

"He's a friend of the family, not my personal friend. I have known him for quite some time, but we have never, ever looked at each other in that light. I mean, not to put any pressure on you, but he's a really good guy. He has a really good job, no kids, and from what I hear, knows how to treat his lady."

Even though Steven fit the appearance to a T of a guy that I would normally date, I really didn't want to venture down the very same route. Just the other day I assured myself that I was changing the stakes and going for men that weren't so visually appealing. However, I couldn't help but take notice to the fact that he had substantial income and no baby mama drama. Even though he may have the stability, as well as the availability, and not to mention the appearance, I would have to take a pass on this one. It was imperative that I switched up my norm or I would continuously be faced with the same outcome every time.

"Well, I'm not sure about Steven; I'm really looking for more of an older guy at this point, who isn't so into his appearance," I replied.

After going back and forth for a while, mainly about Steven, I finally ended the call. I didn't have time to waste discussing things that were not adding to my life. Looks and appearance did not float my boat, and they damn sure don't pay the bills. Although he may have a flow of disposable cash, at least according to Jasmine, I just couldn't risk the possible lack of loyalty.

Within two hours I had made my way to at least seven different stores. My arms were hurting as several bags outlined them from my wrist on up to my elbows. Making my way pass Neiman Marcus, I wanted desperately to go in but I knew that could only be possible if I dropped off a few bags. As I made my way to the car I noticed a familiar looking face coming directly towards me. Peering slightly I tried to determine exactly how I knew this person. And then in an instant it hit me: it was the guy Steven from the party Friday night.

"Hey, stranger," said Steven with a charming yet flirtatious smile.

"Oh, hey there. Again we meet; what are the odds?" I replied with a little hint of sarcasm.

"Yeah, I know, in such close proximity, right? It must be fate."

Deciding not to comment, I continued looking on with a slight smile.

"So, about the other night. I don't know any other way to say this, but from the moment I laid eyes on you I was immediately infatuated. I don't know, it was just something about your smile and the way you carried yourself. Have you talked to Jasmine since that night?" he asked.

"Um, she did mention that you inquired about me, but nothing further," I replied as I slid my shopping bags off my arm and placed them in front of me.

"I mean not to be the guy who sends messages, I have absolutely no problem approaching women, but I was just so taken back by you."

"Is that right?" I asked, giggling inwardly at his cheesy pick up line.

"I mean, yeah, I really couldn't help myself, I just had to let her know how I felt about you; I mean, I didn't want to run the risk of never seeing you again."

As I stood there, I tried to make sense of his proclaimed instant infatuation. Although he was trying to present this uncanny demeanor, his approach just seemed so desperate. Regardless of the fact, I must admit his apparent infatuation gave me an unprecedented thrill. I loved seeing men vie and lust for the opportunity to be a part of my world. It showed me that they were serious and would probably do anything to garner and keep my attention. Like a predator, I was immediately drawn.

"Hmm, okay," I replied intentionally leaving him hanging.

"I mean, are you single or dating?"

"I'm dating," I inserted with a slight look of seriousness.

"Okay, okay, well hopefully at some point you'll be willing to give me a chance. I mean, anybody can tell you that I'm a good guy with good intentions. I just need an equally honest woman by my side as a partner."

And those exact words are just what I wanted to hear. It was just something about having that right man by your side that would make even the biggest problems appear small, and Steven looked great for the picking. He was established, well spoken, and from what I could see, driven. Not to mention the fact that he also appeared seamlessly vulnerable and easily controlled.

"Okay. Well, I'll take your number and we can go from there," I replied.

After giving me his number he insisted that I call him right then and there. It was obvious that he wanted to make sure that he had my number as well. After exchanging numbers we parted ways.

Figuring that I had nothing to lose, I decided that I would give Mr. Steven a shot. He seemed overly infatuated and like the curious cat that I had become, I was anxious to see what he had in store for me. After all, what did I have to lose? Little did he know that once I put my charm down, it would be everything to gain; fuck love, I needed funds.

.

« CHAPTER 4 »

AFTER JUST A COUPLE DAYS back at work, I was anxiously
ready for the weekend—yet again. It's amazing how you can be so
pumped to get into something new and still cringe at the idea of
going to work. I mean, I love what I do and the pay certainly
doesn't disappoint, but it was just something about getting up
every morning and having to actually show up somewhere that
bothered me. Nevertheless, like clockwork, I was always ready to
show up and take charge of my future.

"Hey Leah, there's going to be a management meeting after lunch,
so please make sure that your schedule is clear for this afternoon,"
said Mr. Merlich through the office intercom.

"What time is it exactly?" I asked, annoyed.

"It'll probably be from one to two o'clock; Jenny's still working on
the final details."

"Okay, I'll just try to finish up everything prior to that, just to be
safe."

"Thanks, Leah. Oh, and be sure to bring all of your charts from last
month reports, we'll be going over them in detail," he added.

"Sure thing."

Once the meeting and its logistics were confirmed, I made sure
that my intercom was in the off position. Sitting back in my chair, I
breathed heavily as I fantasized lying on the beach, sipping a

martini. For some reason these sort of visualizations seem to relax me as I prepared for our torturous end of the month meetings.

Merlich did, however, make attempts to make things a little more comical. The thing I like most about him was his ability to maintain his business persona while still being jovial. When he meant business, you just knew it, and when it was time to unwind, you knew it as well. Unlike some other businessmen, he definitely was one that knew how to make his staff feel like part of an extended family, while adequately maintaining that perfect level of professionalism.

Like any other day, I closed a couple deals, answered emails, and consulted with a few clients. Before long I looked up at the clock and it was already time for lunch.

Feeling that I would just grab a snack and prepare for the meeting, I sat at my desk as I began my preparations. As soon as I opened my bag of pistachios, I felt the distinctive feeling of my phone vibrating. Looking down, I realized that it was Steven.

Deciding not to answer, I rejected the call before sending him a text that I would call him a little later on. Almost immediately after sending the text, he replied with an "okay" and that he couldn't wait to see me again.

"Oh boy, he's already showing signs of being a bug," I whispered to myself.

Since the run-in and through just a few conversations, he seems undeniably smitten. I could easily tell that Steven was one of those guys who were simply infatuated with the idea of just being with someone. Deciding to not ponder on it further, I picked up my notes and began reviewing them.

As the day went on, and even through the boring meeting, I continued texting Steven. Through conversation I agreed to take him up on his offer for a dinner date this Friday night. He seemed overly excited, and I must admit that I was as well. However, my intentions were probably not as kosher; I was simply ready to uncover what I had presumably attained.

Getting lost in work, I didn't realize how much time had elapsed. It was almost 5:30 and by the eerie quietness, the office seemed practically empty.

In that very moment, I logged out of my computer and began gathering my things. Feeling a little high spirited, I figured that I would hit up a nice happy hour somewhere before taking it in. And what better person to do that with than Karen? Not to mention the fact that I needed to catch her up on everything that was going on.

"What's up, what's up," said Karen in her usual cheery voice as she answered the phone.

"What's good, B?" I replied, giggling slightly before continuing. "What do you have going on right now; I'm thinking happy hour."

"Girl, you must have read my damn mind. I'm literally sitting here with Josh listening to him talk about bullshit —he's really starting to get on my fucking nerves now."

"Oh God, tell me how I knew this was coming. You are definitely not the one to be held down for too long with one guy."

"Tell me about it, I may have to branch out of this real soon. But what spot did you have in mind?" she asked.

"Ke-Ke's maybe? I hear that spot has a lot of decent guys and the atmosphere is really laid back."

"Well, Ke-Ke's it is."

Once we agreed on a meeting spot, I unlocked my drawer to grab my purse, when suddenly I heard movement in the hallway.

"Still here?" said the voice as I witnessed my office door slowly creep open.

Quickly poking his head in was Merlich.

Holding my chest as I grasped for air, I regained my composure.

"I thought everyone was out of the building, what are you still doing here?" I asked curiously.

"I just had to make sure that a couple deals went through before I left. You know how hesitant clients can become when it's time to put up any money, so I just had to rigor in a little convincing. But now that that's all done, a little birdie just told me that they overheard someone making happy hour plans just a minute ago."

Was this guy some kind of snoop? The conversation was brief as ever and I wasn't even talking that loud. I really hated when people felt the need to dip and dab in my business, and then having the audacity to comment after eavesdropping.

"Was I really talking that loud?" I asked.

"Either that or the walls are really thin," he replied with an animated smile.

No, you're just fucking nosey, I thought inwardly while giving off a similar smile before replying.

"But yeah, I just called up a friend of mine and suggested we do a spot called Ke-Ke's for drinks."

"Oh, is that the new spot that just opened?"

"Yeah, I guess; it is fairly new." I said.

"Yeah well if it is, it's a really nice little spot near the water. Is this like a girls outing or is guys invited?"

"I mean, if you would like to come that's not a problem, the more the merrier," I replied, lying straight through my teeth.

As I continued on with the conversation, I couldn't help but think of how brave and forward my boss had become. I always knew and loved his warm personality, but his forwardness was becoming more and more blatant. He was always overhearing conversations and snooping around the office like some kind of detective. I wouldn't be surprised if he were here on some undercover FBI mission, because that level of nosiness couldn't possibly be an everyday norm.

Before walking out of the office I confirmed with Mr. Merlich that I would meet him at the bar around 6:30. Still not enthused about the intrusion, I decided to suck it up as an extension of the job. The only thing that was going through my mind was the potential male block that he would impose.

Hopping in my car, I sped out of the parking garage within record time. Almost immediately I was faced with the tumultuous evening traffic. As usual, cars were bumper to bumper. Cranking up my R&B playlist, I slipped on my Ray Ban aviators as I made my way near the intercostals.

∞∞∞∞

"Hey mama," I said greeting Karen with a hug.

"Hey, you," she replied.

"Okay now I must warn you, Merlich is going to be here any minute; he practically invited himself."

"Wow, really? You know we have catching up to do," she replied, seemingly annoyed.

"Yeah, I said the same thing, but just this once is okay, I guess. I didn't want to be rude and make him feel unwelcomed. Shhh, here he comes," I quickly added.

"So, this is where the real party animals go?" said Merlich, greeting us before pulling up a chair.

"It's happy hour, baby!" I happily replied in an attempt to uplift the mood.

"Why are you ladies drink-less?" asked Merlich with a knitted look on his face before continuing. "C'mon, lets order a couple rounds of crown and ginger or something."

As we sat at the bar ordering round after round and laughing with Merlich, I could feel myself getting a little too tipsy. Looking down at my watch, I was shocked to see that it was already going on 9:00. Thinking my watch was playing tricks on me I continued staring at it when I felt my phone began to vibrate.

Digging it out of my purse, I realized that it was Steven.

"Hey hun," I replied, a little nicer than usual.

"Hey sweetie. I tried texting you and didn't get a response."

"Really? I must not have heard the phone. It's kind of loud where I am so...."

"Yeah it really is, where are you exactly?" he asked.

"I'm at this spot called Ke-Ke's, can I call you later I can barely hear you."

"Okay sure," replied Steven before ending the call."

After hanging up with Steven, I decided to start taking selfies when I saw a text flash across my screen that read: *Since you're out and about, I really wouldn't mind seeing you tonight. I know we agreed on dinner Friday but I'm not sure I can last that long.*

Giggling to myself, I texted back that I would call him once I left the spot and hopefully we could meet up. Not wanting to stay much longer and risk not being able to drive home, I decided that I would finish my last drink and then head out.

"Leaving?" asked Karen as I stood up.

"Yeah, it's getting kind of late and I already had my fair share of drinks for one night."

"Awe, c'mon. Tomorrow is probably going to be a slow day anyway; come later if you want," added Merlich.

"Like, really," interjected Karen before continuing. "I should be the one leaving early; you're here with your boss."

"Well it's not that, I'm just a little tired, had a really long week."

"Another round," said Merlich to the bartender who had come up to check on us.

"Excuse me, I have to go to the men's room. Karen, pin her down till I get back."

As Merlich turned to leave I looked in Karen's direction. Waiting until he was out of eyesight, I nudged Karen on the shoulder.

"Sooo, what's that about?" I asked curiously.

"What's what about?" replied Karen, blushing slightly.

"C'mon, Karen, I've known you for far too long, you know exactly what I mean. You two were obviously flirting this whole time and the fact that you're not pushing to leave with me seals the deal."

Karen burst out laughing before replying. "Okay, okay, I know that I was talking shit about him coming out with us, but he seems really cool. And let's also mention the fact that he was flirting with me as well."

"You two were flirting with each other; I was sitting there like, 'Did I miss something? Karen seems interested in Merlich?'"

"Well, I've always been attracted to men who are put together. I just managed to get caught up with a few squares and a couple that were from the rougher side of the tracks. But I do like nice men as well, Leah. Damn."

"Hey, I'm not saying something's wrong with it, I'm just shocked more than anything," I replied. "But, hey! It won't be long before he returns and I've got to go handle some business. I'll call you tomorrow and give you the details; and likewise, I need to hear more."

Confirming that I would let her know once I made it home, I speed walked out of the restaurant and headed for the parking lot. As soon as I arrived at my car, my phone began vibrating. Realizing that it was Steven yet again, I confirmed with him that I would be leaving shortly and would meet him at another bar in North Broward.

Immediately upon arriving at the bar, it was obvious that this was one of those spots where Wednesday was one of its hottest nights. Patrons lined the building walls in numbers. Feverishly searching for a parking spot, I noticed several old school cars, as well as a couple others, creeping through the parking lot. As I continued looking around I knew in an instant that this spot wasn't for me.

Picking up my phone I decided to call Steven and see if he had made it.

"Hey, are you here?" I asked.

"I'm about to pull up as we speak, where are you?" he replied.

"I just found a parking spot on the other side of the club; I'll just wait for you here."

Once Steven arrived, we made our way inside the bar. Grabbing a seat at a table, we ordered several rounds of tequila and a couple rounds of Henny and Coke. After just two shots, I could no longer ignore the feeling of my kitty jumping in my panties.

As I continued listening to him speak, I began laser focusing on his lips as I thought about the degree of damage that they could do to me. His lips were a warm pinkish-brown and appeared soft like infant skin. Just looking at them gave me the undying feeling of them going one-on-one with the lips of my punany.

Granted, we just hooked up, but with the amount of alcohol that was now in my system it was becoming more and more difficult to hold in my inner beast. I wanted my pussy licked from the top to the very bottom. I wanted a reason to scream and yell someone's name.

As I continued to look at him I started giving him the eye so that it would be no mistake as to what I was after. Catching my gaze we met eye-to-eye; feeling hypnotized, I wanted desperately for my inner core to be filled. And since no one else was on my list, it would be an undisclosed game of Simon Says, with me as the messenger.

« CHAPTER 5 »

"SO, WHAT HAPPENED LAST night?" asked Karen, staring at me as I lay on the couch.

Struggling to hold my head up I rubbed my eyes as I tried to adjust them to the light.

"Oh God, please tell me why I went on a drinking spree like I was given a set time to live? I feel horrible," I finally replied.

After going to the kitchen and grabbing me a bottle of water, Karen sat beside me on the couch, looking on as I gulped it down to the last drop.

"I'm just trying to figure out what else did you have to drink, because I'm fine and we were practically drinking the same thing all night."

"Well, you know I left and met up with Steven..."

Stopping me mid-sentence, Karen raised her hand. "Wait! Who the hell is Steven?"

After filling her in on the lifestyle party, mall run-in, and subsequent number exchange between Steven and I, I relayed much of what I could remember from the night before.

"Well, thank God you were able to call me to come and get you from the bar. You don't even know buddy well enough to go off binge drinking with him alone."

"I know, and I feel horrible about being so irresponsible. It's like, the last thing I remember is sitting at the bar and just feeling myself dazed and totally wasted. I knew then that I had to leave. I mean, it was actually to the point where I was getting hot and bothered. I could have stripped him and given him the business right then and there," I sighed.

"Well, just thank God your new friend isn't some creep who would take advantage of you," replied Karen.

After talking more about the night, I rested a little further before getting up and heading home. Karen had to go to work and I needed to get my laptop so that I could respond to my long list of emails while preparing for the workday.

During the drive home, I turned off the radio and took the quiet time to collect my thoughts and clear my head. Steven seemed to be a good guy, although he is exactly the kind of guy that I swore to stay away from. But his actions, or should I say inactions, last night definitely gave him bonus points in my book. He was with me during a very vulnerable period and did what any respectable man would do, and that was urge me to call a friend.

But I still refuse to be anyone's fool. Steven earned his points with me and that simply opened me up to dating him, but like a soldier, my mission must continue. Any *situation-ship* that I entered at this point had to be for my betterment, both emotionally and financially.

Before I even realized it, I had made my way home. Pulling up to my condo gave me a sense of security; I was officially safe and sound.

As I walked up the pathway I could see something colorful lying down by the door, but I was unable to make it out from the distance. As I got closer I quickly realized that it was a bouquet of roses with a card attached to it.

Surprised, yet curious, I quickly contemplated on who could possibly be the sender. Who knew where I lived that would randomly be sending me roses? Holding my breath I cracked open the card and read:

> *To: Leah*
>
> *I'm so happy that I found you; you're more beautiful in person than your pictures can ever display. You are indeed special, and hopefully soon I will be able to show you exactly what I mean.*
>
> *Love,*
>
> *Your secret admirer*

I was flabbergasted. Who could have sent me roses with such a heartfelt message? And how did they find my address?

Ramming the key in the lock, I scurried inside as quickly as possible and keyed in my code to the alarm. Noticing that the system had no recent alarms, I breathed a sigh of relief.

The mystery of who my secret admirer could be continued to circle throughout my mind. Determined to get to the bottom of it, I decided to make a couple of phone calls with Jasmine being the first.

"Hey, Ma," answered Jasmine nonchalantly.

"Hey, what's going on?"

"Nothing much, just browsing through the net. What's up with you?"

"Cool. Listen, I just got home and was instantly put on edge. As soon as I got to the doorstep I noticed a bouquet of roses that had a message from a secret admirer. It was short, but stated how beautiful I was in person yada yada and hopefully we will meet soon or something of the sort. I'm so puzzled as to who it could be."

"Secret admirer? Hmm, who have you strung along now?" she asked.

"Nobody! I'm still trying to figure out how this person got my private address."

"Relax. Maybe it's one of your ex's messing with you; or it could be someone new," replied Jasmine.

"Well, it could be Lawrence, but I doubt it. Lawrence has probably moved on by now because I haven't heard from him in a while. Besides he never sent roses like that when were together to begin with. You don't think it's Steven, do you?" I asked curiously. "I mean, I know you have been to my house once, are you sure you didn't slip and let him know where I lived?"

"Not at all. Steven and I haven't talked since the last time he asked about you. I doubt it was him."

Not sure if I should believe her or not, I decided to rest the topic. It seemed apparent that even if she did know something or shared anything about me, she was not going to be forth coming.

 So for now it would just be in my best interest to watch my back and continually check my surroundings. For all I know it could be someone out to get me.

As I sat on the couch probing my mind for possibilities, I began to feel myself drift away. The strong feeling of sleep was simply more than I could bear.

∞∞∞

The next week at work sailed by effortlessly. Since I had caught up on most of my emails the day before, I was way ahead of the eight ball. With two client cancellations, I would practically be free after lunch; and everyone knows free for me essentially means trouble.

Steven has been calling and texting me all day, but I was just too busy trying to wrap up the day to attend to any forms of outside communication.

It's actual nice to have a guy in my life that seems to generally care for reasons more than his own sexual gratification. Steven has the characteristics of a protector and warrior. Maybe this is the universe's way of rewarding me for the loyalty and good that I have put out over the past few years. I just hate that I met him at this point in my life.

Rising from my desk, I logged off of the computer and closed the blinds behind me. Slightly straightening up my files, I prepared my paperwork and charts as if I wouldn't be back until Monday; and the way that things can be with me, I probably wouldn't.

As I headed out of the office, I waved at the front desk clerk Claire before informing her to hold all of my messages until I returned. Confirming that she would, I walked out of the double doors, jumping on the elevator and down towards freedom.

The moment I made it outside of the building, the sunrays hit me instantaneously. Scurrying to my car, I hopped in and took off towards the interstate. Since I hadn't seen my sister in a while, I figured I would make a stop by my parent's house. Besides, this was my sister's last summer at home and it was paramount that we spent a little time together before she leaves. She needed to know the ends and outs of this dirty, cold world.

Even though my life hadn't turned out so badly, I still didn't want my sister making unfortunate mistakes; especially when it came to dating. She needed to be put on game, and who better to teach her than her big sister. Deciding to just get my food to- go, I called in my order.

While making my way to the restaurant, I decided to call up Steven to see what he had going on for the night. He mentioned that he had no plans and would love it if he could spend some time with me. In agreement, we decided on a game of bowling at the new location off Brickell.

As I pulled up to my parent's house, I noticed my mom's car was parked in an unusual spot with my sister's car right behind it.

That's strange. Mom never parks there, I thought to myself.

Pushing my key through the hole, I quietly entered the house like a burglar making her move. A BOOM! sound rang out.

Emerging from behind the door, laughing hysterically, was my goofy little sister, Mia.

"Oh my God, Mia, you could have given me a heart attack; don't do that!" I yelled while holding my hand to my chest.

"Relax, I was only playing around," she replied through constant laughter before continuing.

"Why are you so uptight and on edge?"

"I'm not you just caught me off guard. Where is everybody?" I asked.

"Well, Dad's at the office, duh, and Mom went out with Carol to go shopping, I guess."

"If she's with Carol, she won't be coming home anytime soon. And why is her car parked the way it is?"

"I have no idea."

As soon as I started making my way toward the hallway, Mia's entire demeanor changed. She had a flushed look on her face and I knew in an instant that something was up.

"Oh, did you put up the picture frame I gave you for your birthday?" I asked as I edged closer to my destination.

"Um, no! And my room isn't clean, so don't go in there."

Pretending to adhere to her request I casually continued walking. Appearing as if I was going to walk past her door, I quickly jolted backward and immediately grabbed the doorknob.

Pushing it open, I noticed nothing unusual until something caught the corner of my eye. After a few seconds of staring it being evident that there was in fact something or someone in the bed. Looking back at Mia, I gave her the look that meant I wanted answers. Remaining quiet, she looked at me with no expression.

As I edged closer towards the bed, I braced myself for what I could possibly uncover. Hastily making one quick tug at the comforter, I was instantly greeted with an unusual yet mysterious looking face staring squarely back at me.

« CHAPTER 6 »

CONTINUING TO STARE IN CONFUSION, I analyzed his face keenly trying to remember how and if I knew him. After a few seconds, and to no avail, I turned my head towards Mia with my eyebrows raised and a confused look on my face.

"Okaaay?" I finally managed to say before continuing. "Can someone please tell me what's going on here?"

"Well, I'm Justin, and a friend of Mia's."

"Justin?" I asked.

"For some reason you look really familiar. Do I know you from somewhere?" I asked curiously as Mia stood off in the distance not saying a word.

"Well, I'm not sure. I mean, I don't think I've ever seen you before, but you know what they say, everyone has a twin," he replied with an uncanny smile.

It was just something about him, something that gave me the creeps. His facial expressions, the way he smiled, the way he looked at me, and even the way he talked just sent chills up and down my spine. Knowing that I had at least seen him somewhere before, I leered in on his face as I was hoping to implant it in my mind. If I knew him, and certain that I do, it will eventually come back to me when I least expect it.

"Yeah, that's what they say, huh," I replied nonchalantly.

Nodding in agreement he continued to smile and stare.

"Can I speak to you for a second?" I said, turning to Mia.

Rolling her eyes, she breathed heavily before walking out of the room. Making our way outside, I slammed the door in frustration.

"What the hell do you think you're doing?" I yelled.

"What do you mean, what am I doing? He's just a friend that I hang out with."

"Just a friend you hang out with? This guy doesn't even look like he's near your age. Where the hell did you meet him and how old is he!" I yelled.

"Leah, look, I'm a grown ass woman, and I have the choice to converse with whoever I like. What does it matter how old he is?" replied Mia, appearing to become agitated.

"I asked you a question?" I replied sternly, making sure that I made eye contact.

"36!" she finally replied.

"36? Mia you do not need someone who is damn near twice your age. You need to have your mind on getting ready for college right now. Not lying up with some old ass creep!"

Staring at me with squinted eyes and a knitted up mouth, I began to see fury in her eyes.

"Oh I see exactly what this is about! You can't stand to see me with someone and you not have anyone. You're mad because your ass is lonely and I have a guy who is into me."

"Excuse me?"

"Yeah, you heard me. Enough is enough. You think everything should always be about you. If Leah isn't happy, no one should be happy. If Leah isn't dating, no one should be dating. Leah should always be the spotlight, the golden child. Well I have news for you, times have changed, and so have I," Mia said with defiance in her voice.

Staring at her in utter shock, I was simply at a loss for words. Is this how my sister truly felt throughout the years? Did we not get equal love and attention from both of our parents?

"So, because I'm calling you out on your bullshit, you want to turn things around on me? Mia, save it! I have never tried to make things all about me, so I'm warning you right now, be careful what you say, because you can't take words back."

"I've said what I had to say and I'm done with it. That guy that you saw in there takes care of me. Whatever I want, it's never a question; I get it. So what if I want to have a little fun before I leave? Let me live; you did!"

As I continued staring at my little sister, I knew deep down inside that something wasn't right. What happened to the person who took heed to my advice? Here I am thinking that it's time to have our little talk, while she's already set on veering left before she can even experience life. Just from the way he looked, I knew that he was not the right person for her. Mia had very little experience with dating, let alone dating an older guy who appeared to be from the rougher side of the tracks.

"You know what? I'm going to just leave, because it's clear that you have lost your damn mind and I'm going to hold off until you find it. You're acting like some underprivileged hood rat that is in need of a sponsor. What can he give you that Mom and Dad haven't?

What is it that you are so desperately in need of? Huh, Mia? Tell me, what is it?" I asked.

"Dick!"

∞∞∞

Jumping up at the sound of the alarm caused me to groan in agony. Then almost in an instant I remembered that it was only Friday night and the alarm was for my date with Steven. As I continued lying in bed, the earlier incident with Mia came rushing through my mind. It truly hurt me to hear my sister talk the way that she had. While one part of me wanted to just strangle her, the other part of me felt like it was an outlet for deeper pain. It had to be something that she was missing that she was in search for. Luckily she would be leaving soon and this guy by all accounts will hopefully be a faded memory, so with that in mind I decided to not ponder on it further. At this point, all I can do is talk to her and school her on what's out there. What she does with the advice is totally up to her.

Finally deciding to get out of bed, I rummaged through my closet before I decided on an olive colored romper, paired with my tan Valentino pumps and a multicolored Jimmy Choo clutch that I picked up the other day.

After showering, laying my hair, and applying make-up, I was ready for the nightlife.

Cruising through traffic gave me a sense of enthusiasm. Granted, it was Friday night and most people were probably out in their weekend mode, but it was still so apparent that people from south Florida were without a doubt about their money. If we had to hustle trail mix on the side of the road, that's what we did until better came along. We made it happen and for that very reason alone I had madd love for my city.

Lost in thought, I didn't realize that I had reached my destination. Pulling up, I immediately texted Steven to let him know that I had arrived. Quickly texting back, he relayed to me that he was at the bar waiting.

Once inside the bowling alley, the first person that caught my eye was Steven, as our eyes met head on.

"Sorry I'm late; you know this weekend traffic can be a mess," I said, greeting him before taking a seat.

"It's okay, you're worth the wait," said Steven, smiling as he took a sip of his drink.

Smiling back, I squirmed in my seat as I tried getting comfortable.

 "So, how was your day, babe?" he asked.

"Well, work was work, but overall the day went well."

"Good," replied Steven, before continuing. "So, what had you in such a grunt earlier when I called?"

"Oh geesh, my freaking little sister. I don't know what's gotten into her; I think it may just have to do with the stress of going off to college," I replied.

Not wanting to get back into story, but being urged to do so, I gave Steven a briefing of what actually happened. It was refreshing talking to Steven and getting an outside view from someone in a some-what neutral state. He seemed to understand how I felt, and where I was coming from. Continuing to talk as much as we drank, Steven assured me that everything would be okay and that she was probably just experiencing the growing pains.

After hanging out at the bar a little longer, we proceeded to the hosting station to pick up socks, shoes, and lane information.

As we bowled, drank, and laughed at each other's mistakes, I began feeling relaxed as I started looking at Steven in another light. He was in fact not that bad of a person. He appeared humorous, compassionate, and especially attentive.

Which really made me wonder why he was single. It's no military secret that there is in fact a shortage of good men willing to take on the needed role, so the fact that he was a free agent plagued my curiosity. Determined to enjoy things until shown otherwise, I put my wondering thoughts to the back of my mind.

"I need to take a potty break; I've been holding it for a minute now," I said to Steven before walking back to the sitting area.

"Go ahead, I'll be right here prepping for another butt whooping, and don't try to go Google any last minute tips now," he replied jokingly.

After flushing the toilet, I stopped short in front of the mirror to make sure that everything was on point. Applying additional lip gloss and running blot powder over my face brought me right back to life. Cheesing in the mirror, I inwardly admired myself. Despite the wheel of pretty girls that were often seen in Miami, it was no doubt that I was one of the elite. My teeth, skin, hair, wardrobe, and personality set me apart from the has-beens and the wannabes. Though humble, at least in my opinion, I was damn good at being me.

Immediately upon stepping out of the restroom hallway, I felt someone grab a hold of my hand. Flashing my head to the right I was confronted by a tall, yet chunky guy with an almond colored tan.

"My apologies if I frightened you, but my boss would like to have a word with you," he added with a serious look on his face, barely opening his mouth.

"Actually, you did. And what boss?" I asked while pulling away from his grasp.

Letting go and staring briefly he continued. "Again, my apologies, I often times forget my level of strength. If you come right this way, I can better explain to you who he is. He noticed you as you played and would just like to have a word with you, is that alright?" he asked in a foreign, English sounding accent.

"Well, can't he meet us here? I'm not sure if I want to follow you."

"He's in a private room and feels a little more comfortable in a private setting; we also noticed that you were with someone," the stranger said.

Feeling a little more assured due to the setting being relatively public, I decided to go and see exactly who was this boss that had other men doing his dirty work. Turning slightly to see if Steven was watching, I quickly turned back around to give the messenger the okay.

Walking towards the back of the bowling alley, I prayed silently that Steven didn't notice me and my unusual deterrence. As we made our way to the room my heart pounded uncontrollably. Not knowing what I was walking into or what to expect gave me an immediate rush.

Pulling back the velvet curtain, the stranger invited me to go inside.

Quickly peering inside, yet still behind the worker, I witnessed an older looking man sitting in a lounge chair holding a drink. Standing beside him was another buff looking guy who I assumed was another worker. Sitting on a red-colored love seat were two blonde haired females with their legs crossed and two martini-looking drinks in their hands.

With all attention now geared towards me, I swallowed hard before finally stepping inside; unsure as to exactly what I had gotten myself into.

« CHAPTER 7 »

"WELL HELLO, BEAUTIFUL," said the foreign speaking man as he sipped brown liquid out of a long tapered glass.

"Hello," I replied, trying desperately not to sound nervous.

"I hope I didn't frighten you, I simply had to get your attention."

So much for that, I thought to myself as I looked on. It became increasingly clear that this guy was in fact a boss. He boasted a navy blue suit with a plain white dress shirt that exposed a portion of his chest. His hair was jet black and neatly swept to the side. Sitting on his wrist was a plain, chrome colored watch that without question was sure to be expensive.

"Well, not really I'm more curious than anything at this point," I replied smiling nervously.

"Don't worry, you're in good hands; it's the bad guys that you should be afraid of," he quickly added. "Have a seat; I would like to chat with you for a bit."

Slowly walking in, I noticed he said something to the guy on his right before he walked away. Nervously taking a seat beside him, I pondered on what to say.

"The name is Chanlor, and it is more than a pleasure to meet you," he continued as he stuck out his hand.

"Leah, Leah Miller," I replied, realizing that I had mistakenly said my entire name.

Graciously taking my hand he lowered his face and kissed it.

"You are a very nice looking woman, I must say."

"Why, thank you, and you're not too bad yourself," I replied.

What the hell was up with my responses? Never in a million years have I uttered such corny comebacks. What was wrong with me? Was he exerting that much of an influence on me so soon?

"What do you like to drink? I'll have the bartender whip you up something; whatever it is, just name it."

"Umm, I'm okay, actually."

It would be just my luck that the entire drink would end up on me instead of in me. Besides, Steven was outside waiting and it would look suspicious if I left for as long as I did and returned back with a drink.

 Unsure of what I had gotten myself into, I pondered on what excuse I would use to leave. I didn't like the feeling that he was giving me, nor did I like my uncontrollable nervousness while in his presence. Clearly I had gotten in way over my head and was fiddling with the bass of the sea. Never one to back down at a challenge, however, I was gradually feeling captivated by his smooth yet sly charm.

"Not much of a drinker, I see," he causally replied as he took a sip of his drink.

"Well, I drink here and there, but I'm here with the family and I try not to drink too much when I'm around them."

"I see, I see. Well that's understandable," he added before continuing, "Since you're here with family it would be selfish of me to continue to hold you up; my man here will give you my information and we can presumably go from there. Oh, and make sure that I hear from you soon, I think the two of us will have heaps of fun together. Even better, just write your name on one of the cards so that I can know what number to expect."

Immediately after the words left his mouth, the bodyguard that was standing beside him came over and handed me two cream colored business cards.

After writing my name and number, I handed it back to the buffed up servant.

"Well, it was really nice meeting you," I said as I turned back to Chanlor.

"The pleasure was all mine, my dear," he replied with a sexy yet deviant smile.

As I was getting up to leave I was hit with a loathing ray of jealous stares. If looks could kill, the two bird looking blondes would have murdered me in an instant. Little did they know that unwarranted jealousy was like ammunition in my world. Gracefully perfecting my walk, I strutted out of the room like the diva I was known to be.

Wishing I had stayed, I became inwardly giddy about my short, yet interesting encounter.

"You had me worried there for a minute, I almost came looking for you," said Steven as he sat on the seat near the bowling lane.

"I'm sorry, sweetie, I was yapping away in the ladies room with the attendant. I didn't realize that it was the mom of an old friend until we started talking."

"Yeah, I know how that can be when two ladies get together," he replied as he shook his head in confirmation.

"You know, just catching up. So where were we?" I swiftly added in an attempt to switch subjects.

The more we continued to sip and bowl, the sexier Steven became. Before long I looked at my watch and it was already going on one thirty in the morning.

"Are you ready to go?" I asked.

"Yeah, I'm kind of ready to leave here, but I'm not sure if we should end the night this early."

"Well, what else do you have in mind?" I asked.

"Nothing in particular, let's just get in my car and do something spontaneous. Hell, it's Friday night, the actual nightlife is just getting started."

Tipsy and feeling quite the same, I agreed to extend the night. Hopping in his car we sped off towards the interstate.

After driving around for thirty minutes or so, we finally were able to agree on the South Beach area, as it would afford us the option of bars and clubs, as well as the privacy of the beach.

"It's a really nice night tonight," I said, gazing up at the stars.

"Very. No rain, not too humid; the epitome of perfect," he replied.

"So, why did you want to come here?" I finally decided to ask.

Breathing in the night's air before slowly exhaling, he looked over at me before responding.

"No reason in particular, just some one-on-one time. Seems like ever since we met we've always been in the mix of other people."

"Well, that's typically how the first few dates normally go," I replied in a humorous yet sarcastic tone.

"Yeah, I know, but I just want to be close to you. You know, face to face; just us."

Sitting on the sand we talked about everything under the sun, or should I say moon. He discussed his childhood, family life, and how he got to this point in life. Though not initially interested, I slowly became intrigued. His mother was never there because of drug use and prostitution, and his father was never even in the picture to begin with. Having two absentee parents caused him to bounce around from house to house, mostly relatives, until he reached the age of eighteen, when he was then left to fend for himself.

Just hearing his story and the struggle that he had to endure to get to where he is now made me proud of him, and also appreciate the family that I had. He appeared to be someone who never experienced real love and was still desperately trying to find it.

Infused with alcohol while sitting next a handsome specimen under a starry night was definitely a recipe for disaster. Listening to his story made me want to love him, yet I didn't want to take on the responsibility of having to make up for unfortunate past times. So for now, all that I can give him is what I originally planned to offer. Nothing more, nothing less.

As he continued talking, I slowly began leaning forward. The moment our lips connected sent vibrations throughout my entire body. Kissing him slowly as I took shallow yet heated breaths caused the moment to be all the more magical.

As thoughts of regret began to circle my mind, I consciously blocked them as the need to fulfill my sexual desires immediately overshadowed. It had been far too long since my last enjoyable escapade and like a caged bird, I needed to be set free.

Grabbing the sides of my face as he continued kissing me showed me that he also wanted much of the same. Before long his hands were on my breasts as he fondly began rubbing them. Replicating his actions, I slowly ran my hand across the front of his pants, causing an instant stiffness to protrude—it was as if I summoned it to attention. Just running my fingers alongside his dick confirmed my greatest fears: the package inside felt like nothing less than a monster.

Refusing to engage in drawn out foreplay, I aggressively searched for the top of his zipper before pulling it down. Following my lead he unbuckled his pants and hastily pulled them halfway past his thighs. The very moment I came in contact with his dick caused my eyes to widen and my heart to flutter. Steven's dick was long and thick, with veins that appeared to be on steroids.

"Pull down your jumpsuit."

Hesitating slightly, I zipped down the front of my romper, causing it to quickly fall to my knees. The fact that we were in a public setting quickly added to the thrill, as my desires increased with the mere thought of just getting caught in the act.

"Let's not waste anymore time, give me the condom and sit back," I immediately ordered.

Following my command, Steven positioned himself in the sand to accommodate my straddling body. Hovering over him, I grabbed the head of his penis as I wiggled on it in rhythmic yet sensual motions, urging my juices to commemorate the occasion.

Rising slightly, I slowly slid all the way down on his dick, squeezing it with my pussy muscles as I adjusted myself to the size and feeling. The more I squeezed, the deeper he breathed as his eyebrows knitted up in undeniable pleasure. Clenching my teeth as I buried my feet deeper and deeper in the sand, I continued bouncing and rocking back and forth outwardly begging for the moment to never end. Engulfed in the feeling, I felt the immediate onset of an orgasm.

"Oh shit, I'm about to come!" said Steven as he opened his mouth in a dazed look.

"Oh yes! Yes baby, let me have it!" I yelled as my own orgasm radiated throughout my body. The level of euphoria was more than I could bear. Almost immediately, Steven's entire body became tense as he squeezed my waist and gritted his teeth. Within seconds I could feel his manhood slowly soften inside of me.

And just like that, my mission was complete. Staring into his eyes I knew that I had just fucked up his entire world. The look on his face said it all: he was hypnotized hook, line, and sinker.

« CHAPTER 8 »

OVER THE NEXT FEW WEEKS, Steven and I have spent more and more time with each other—and I must admit that things so far have been great. Sometimes I feel like one day someone will wake me up and it'll all be a dream. He was just more of gentlemen than I thought he would ever be. There is nothing that I ask of him that is not given to me. He refers to me as his queen, and relayed to me on several occasions that he believes we are long lost soul mates that finally found each other. And in all actuality the chemistry cannot be denied; in just a few short dates it feels like I have known him for years, and even if things don't work out I hope that we can at least remain friends.

Things have still been on a downward spiral with my sister and me, and all because of some washed up street thug. Just the knowledge of knowing that she's fro locking around town with him still has me on edge. Even though I can't recall exactly where I know him from, his vibes alone scream bad news. The look on his face and the way he squints his eyes just makes my stomach do flips. And to add insult to injury, my parents have no idea that she's bringing boys into the house, or should I say men. I just hope that she gets some thicker skin on her head once she heads off to school. At least then she'll be surrounded with like-minded individuals that will hopefully help steer her straight.

With Karen being consumed with her new love interest and now Merlich, I have been pretty much left to vent to Steven about all of my life troubles. And like the doting lover he has become, he has always been there for me, if not just as a listening ear. With all the drama going on with my sister, he understands how it feels to love someone and them not understand the authenticity of that love.

The guy Chanlor that I met a couple weeks ago at the bowling alley seems to be a Ken doll on a white horse. He is a widely respected man in the UK and owns several successful businesses.

We have talked over the phone on several occasions and I couldn't be more intrigued. His charm, power, and poise are undeniably sexy. Just one week after meeting him he wired $2,000 through Western Union for me to handle any extra expenses. Though grateful for the small gesture, I was ready to see what else was left to siphon, at least before the well ran dry.

Knowing that he lived in another country, I was not going to sit around and play the lovey-dovey role and not get my cash. In a moment's time it could all be gone—all that needs to happen is for him to see another pretty face and POOF, show ended. So I was going to make damn sure that if and when it did, I would come out with a bank roll that would make high-end escorts look like low-income street workers; this time it would be Leah that got the last laugh.

Coming back to the now, it was a beautiful Saturday morning and time for me to start my day. Remembering that Steven and Jasmine invited me to a party tonight, I knew that my time would be limited before being forced to embark on another wild night.

Agreeing to meet up with Steven beforehand, I prepared myself for the unexpected. At anytime he was known to switch up the plans and venture into something different.

The moment I heard my phone ring I knew that it was Steven calling for me to come outside. Grabbing my phone and bag, I strutted outside to his awaiting car.

"You look nice," said Steven with a wide smile as I got inside the car.

"Thank you, I try my best," I replied, returning his smile before continuing, "So, where are we headed? I couldn't even decide on what to wear due to your unpredictability."

"Uh huh, I keep you on edge, huh?"

"You know you do. I just never know what to expect, which isn't necessarily a bad thing, I must say."

"It's actually funny that you say that because I did in fact have plans for us today, but some things ended up having to be canceled, so we're going to have to reschedule that for a later time," he stylishly replied before continuing. "So, I figured now we could just hit the mall and grab a few things."

"Oh great, my favorite pastime!" I instantly replied.

"I would have never guessed that one."

It didn't matter how much money I had, there was nothing like spending someone else's. And I knew for fact that anytime I went out with Steven, everything was always tailored.

After pulling up to the mall, we got out and devised a game plan. We would hit up his stores first and then mine. His argument was that my shopping would take longer and should therefore be left for last; agreeing yet disagreeing, I continued on with the plan.

Steven was in and out of two department stores in record-breaking time. He went in, saw what he wanted, and quickly paid for them.

"Okay, so I have one last store that I want to visit before you can take the lead," said Steven as we walked out of the second store.

Moments later we entered a huge men's store that had the appearance of a warehouse. It was filled with various designer brands, with a little mix of everything in between. Slow walking behind Steven, I decided to check out what they had to see if I could put together any styling ideas as a little surprise.

As I walked through the rows I admired the quality of the brands that the store carried. Somehow the clothes seemed to remind me of Charles. The way they were neatly arranged and put together seemed like work that would be contributed to him. Grazing aimlessly through the aisles, I was suddenly stopped in my tracks by a strong deep voice.

"Looking for something in particular?" asked the voice.

Turning around I was greeted by a glistening smile.

"Um no, just browsing," I replied somewhat caught off guard.

He was standing inches away from me and was nothing less than edible. Though average in height, he had impeccable facial features with smooth island-looking skin. His facial hair was dark black and smooth—cut and lined like he just hopped out of the barber's chair. Hanging around his neck was a blazing gold chain that reflected perfectly off his skin; though handsome, he was exactly the kind of guy that I swore myself against.

"Do you work here?" I asked curiously.

"No, but I saw you and was wondering what a pretty girl like yourself is doing here alone; are you shopping for your man or something?"

"Well no, I'm here with a family friend helping him find something for his date tonight."

I'm really getting this lying thing down to a science, I thought to myself.

"Oh okay, that's what's up."

After standing quietly for a couple seconds, he continued. "By the way my name is Seth is it okay if I give you my number? I would love to take you out sometime."

"Hmm. Why not?" I said.

Looking around I noticed that Steven was at the register, so I had only mere moments to complete the transaction.

Once I put my number in his phone and said my goodbye, Steven was walking down the aisle with his eyes making direct contact.

"What was that about?" asked Steven the moment he walked up.

"What was what about?" I answered evasively.

"The guy back there, you know him from somewhere?"

"Oh buddy? Nah, he was asking for a woman's advice on some pieces he picked up," I wittily replied.

Still looking suspicious but finally shrugging it off, he said nothing further. As long as he didn't catch me actually giving him my number, then like Shaggy, it wasn't me. There was no way that I was going to carry on with the topic and get him into the habit of questioning me.

After hitting just two stores, I had already spent well over $2,500—and the way that Steven was looking when everything was being rung up said it all. It was if he wanted to pass out when the cashier said the final total. Knowing that his pockets really weren't that deep, I decided to spare him the added agony and take it to the house.

The drive home quickly became awkwardly silent, leaving me to wonder what he was thinking.

"So, what's on your mind?" I finally decided to ask.

"Ahh, just thinking about a few things that happened at work this week."

"Care to share?"

"Well, it's nothing serious, just minor bullshit that happened with a sponsor."

Deciding not to question him any further, I remained silent for the remainder of the car ride. I truly hoped that he was not contemplating on the measly two bands he just got rid of. And now that I think about it, that's probably what it is—which is exactly why I have no desire to entertain low budget men. Volunteer to take me shopping and then shit your pants when the bill comes—yup, he can go on with that; I'm good.

"Okay, here we are," said Steven as we pulled up to my condo.

"Yeah, I got to get in here and do a couple things before it's time to get dressed. What time do you plan on going to the party?" I asked out of curiosity.

"I'll probably get here around ten, if that's good with you," he replied.

"Ten is perfect."

"Could you pop the trunk so I can get my bags, please?"

"Sure," he replied, hopping out of the car.

"I know you didn't think I was going to have you carry these bags, did you?"

Forcefully smiling, I continued down the sidewalk.

Once inside, we kissed briefly before he decided to leave.

Knowing that I didn't have much time left before the party, I immediately retreated upstairs, bags and hangers in tow.

∞∞∞

"My God, this place is packed. Where the hell did all these people come from?" I asked as I gazed slowly around the room.

"Yeah it gets like this sometimes, depending on who's throwing the party. I haven't seen it like this in a while," replied Steven as we made our way deeper inside.

The deeper I got inside the house the more I realized that this was definitely one of those nights where things got real. The party hadn't even kicked off officially and there were pornos playing on every TV, while most of the women walked around in lingerie. The scene was all too familiar, yet still frightening.

"Okay, I'm just letting you know right now that I am not participating in any play. You can go have a little fun if you want, but I'm staying down here to drink and socialize," I said.

"Wow, just push me off. Damn," replied Steven before continuing, "But I'm not really with it tonight myself. Besides, the only way that I would get into anything is if it's with you. And that reminds me, there's something that I want to talk to you about."

"What is it?" I asked curiously, reflecting back to the incidents of the day.

"I'll get to it later."

"Really, Steven, that's going to drive me crazy all night. We might as well leave the party now because my mind is going to go on wondering."

"Relax. My God, I'll tell you later, it's not that big of a deal."

"Well, I know me and I really don't want to ruin the night, so let's just go outside and have a little talk."

As we turned to leave, a weird looking woman suddenly appeared in front of us.

"I know you're not dipping in and out like that, Mr. Steven!" said the weird looking lady with a failed attempt at being sexy.

"No, no, no, just going outside for a sec, we'll be right back," replied Steven.

"Okay now, I'm going to be looking for y'all."

"I'm sorry. Tasha, this is Leah and, Leah, this is Tasha. Tasha is like an Ole-G to the lifestyle, as well as a really good friend of mine," added Steven.

"Hello," I said greeting her with a smile.

"Nice to meet you," the lady replied.

Eager to leave her presence, I tapped Steven on the small of his back as a cue to keep it moving. He immediately ended the conversation and reiterated to her that he would return.

"Where the hell is Jasmine?" I asked as I scanned the area for the car.

"That's right, where is she? I know it doesn't take that long to fix make-up," added Steven, looking around.

 "Oh well, maybe she came inside and we missed her," I said before continuing, "So, no more delays, I'm overly curious as to what you need to talk to me about. Is everything okay with your job? What exactly is going on?"

"The job is a whole other story. One I really don't care to talk about right this minute," said Steven. "What I really wanted to talk to you about could have waited, but since you insist…. I just want to step our sex game up, I'm…"

I cut him off.

"Okay, Steven, not to cut you off, but I think I know where this is going. You want a threesome and I'm going to let you know right now that it is not my forte."

Chucking slightly, he starred at me as if what I was saying something unusual.

"That mouth of yours, I tell you, is nothing short of comical—but it actually makes what I'm going to say even easier. As you know, I control a lot of things at my job and I'm constantly being forced to make split second decisions and take the lead on almost everything. Anyway, I've been having the desire for quite some time now to take on more of a submissive role. In short, and to no longer beat around the bush, I would love for you to be my master."

"As in bondage?" I asked in disbelief.

"Yes. So are you in?"

Staring at him in disbelief, I stood there unable to talk, yet alone move.

"Hello, are you there?" he said, waving his hands back and forth in front of me.

"I mean, I don't know what to say, you really caught me off guard with this one," I finally answered. "Oh gosh, Steven. I don't... definitely not here, though," I continued with my brows knitted up in confusion.

"No, no, no, not here. It's just that I see the warrior in you. You're always taking the lead and you just have that boss like attitude that turns me on."

After letting his request marinate for a moment, it all made sense. Thinking back, every time that we had sex Steven would always want me to do certain things and take on the leading role. Unbeknownst to me, it was all part of his hidden sensual desires. Assuring him that I had to sleep on it and would let him know, we didn't speak much more on the topic. We began making our way back inside the party.

Coming back to the party displayed much of the same. The house was so packed that there was little to no walking room. As we made our way through the crowd en route to the drink table, we were stopped short by Jasmine, speaking briefly before parting ways.

After getting our drinks and muddling through the crowd, we made our way to the back of the house where the second half of the party seemed to be taking place.

"Hey, my man, it's almost that time; how about those Raiders?" yelled a man as he approached Steven.

"Tony, my man, what's going on? Long time no see," replied Steven as the two greeted each other with a macho fist pound.

Standing beside him and listening on, I slowly began scanning the room to see if I could spot Jasmine again. As I inwardly criticized a few of the guests for their elaborate choice of attire, my eyes stopped short of one guest in particular. In that moment it was if my eyes were deceiving me. Blinking several times, I protruded my head forward in an attempt to extend my viewing field. As my shoulders fell backwards and the disappointment set in, I could no longer deny what was right before my eyes.

Laughing and mingling in the kitchen as if nothing was going on, was Mia and her scumbag of a boyfriend.

« CHAPTER 9 »

As I CONTINUED STANDING NEAR the back of the house, my feet began to feel like cement, as I was unable to move. As my heart continued pounding, the ringing of my ears seemed to drown out the music that was only feet away from me. After what felt like almost an eternity, a surge of energy mixed with anger blazed through my body as I leaped from the patio and marched straight towards the glass sliding door.

"Mia, what the hell are you doing here!" I yelled aloud.

Turning around quickly, Mia opened her eyes widely in apparent equal disbelief.

After mere seconds of odd silence, a smirk slowly spread across her face.

"What are you doing here? So you're following me now!" shouted Mia.

As I continued looking on at her, it became apparent that she was under some type of influence. Knowing that my sister barely even drank I knew that it was the doings of someone else.

"Mia, I'm going to ask you again what are you doing here and what the hell have you had to drink?" I continued assertively, lowering my voice as to not make a scene.

"The same reason you're here. Are you taking the place of Mom now? Like I told you before, I don't need you or anyone else checking me for the shit I do; damn, let me live."

"Let you live! You're at a damn lifestyle party half dressed, apparently drunk, and with someone you barely freaking know, and your response to me is let you live!"

"Look, Mia is grown and can make her own decisions, so don't try to mess up our night with your own insecurities," replied her scumbag boyfriend.

"Now wait a minute, this has nothing to do with you! This is a conversation between me and my sister, so get your tired, no good ass out of my face!"

Just as he appeared to be moving towards me, Steven came out of nowhere and jumped directly in between us.

"Hold on, homie, I know you weren't going to charge at her. I will, and I repeat will, turn this party out if you even think about moving," added Steven angrily.

"Oh, don't worry, homeboy, you already know what the play is going to be with you," said the scumbag in assertive monotone.

Almost immediately, several men and women jumped in between the group of us, yelling simultaneously that they didn't want any drama at their party.

After exchanging a few more words, Steven, Jasmine, and I finally agreed to leave. As we walked through the door, I looked back towards Mia's direction as tears began to fill my eyes. Standing there as if nothing had just happened was Mia and her new co-conspirator, making out like two teenagers in heat. Turning around briskly, I scurried out of the house and ran to the car.

"Leah, it's going to be okay. Come here, babe," said Steven as he reached out for a hug.

"Yeah, Leah, I really hate that everything went down like it did; maybe the two of you should just have a sit-down," added Jasmine before continuing, "But I'm confused, what's the beef with you and Justin?"

"You know him!" I quickly added as I pulled away from Steven.

"Yeah, you remember Justin don't you? You guys were talking to each other at one of the parties."

As I stood there reflecting on Jasmines words, I pondered on whether she had me mistaken for someone else. I had only attended a handful of parties, and although he looked familiar, I don't remember seeing him at any of them.

And suddenly like a slap in the head, it finally hit me.

"Son-of-a-bitch!" I blurted out. "I remember him now! That was the pedophile looking bastard that gave me the creeps at that one party I attended with Charles. I knew that I knew him from somewhere, I just couldn't quite put my finger on it. I remember him clearly now, and how just talking to him gave me the freaking goose bumps."

"Yeah, at times he can be a little weird, but from what I hear he has a couple girls that are known to turn tricks for him," added Jasmine.

"What!"

As Jasmine went on to share everything that she knew, I became more and more disgusted. This guy was obviously a sex-craved womanizer that preyed on the young, or whomever he felt was vulnerable. It appears that he is widely known and respected throughout Miami, but very few knew his exact means of business.

As Jasmine continued talking, it became all the more apparent that Justin was in fact very bad news. I knew that his intentions were not loyal and that my sister had unknowingly bit off more than she could chew. How could I help her get out of this, if at all? How could I save the little sister that doesn't even know that she's lost?

As the tears began to flow once again, I dropped my head in Steven's arms as I pondered on what to do next.

∞∞∞

For the next two weeks I seemed to be venturing through a fuzzy haze. Although I tried as hard as I could to not think about it, my sister was constantly on my mind; my guarding personality just wouldn't let me let go of it. My parents would be devastated if they knew the bullshit that Mia was up to. Being the youngest and closest relative to her, it became my inherent mission to guide her out of this very bad situation. Until she leaves for college, I will be on her harder than an army recruiter seeking candidates. I'm going to make it my business to remind her day and night about the bullshit that goes on in these streets, and how one small mistake can ruin your life forever.

Yet again, helping me through my distress was Steven. He was always a listening ear and did everything that he could to make sure that I was okay. With Steven around I felt spoiled. If I asked for it, he broke his neck to make it happen, even if he lacked the resources; which sometimes I felt he did. Things with him were starting to become almost like an obsession. It's as if I am air to him and vital for his survival. Though strange and rather fanatic, I kind of enjoy having someone at my disposal, willing to bend to my every need. His desires to be controlled and dominated seem to be present in his everyday life; whenever I would talk down to him he would get aroused and giddy, like a kid in a candy store. Strange, but nonetheless, interesting.

Outside of Steven, my dating life was really starting to be on the up and up. The money from Chanlor was continuous, and not to mention handy. Talking to him and having the constant flow of money made me feel comfortable, as if money was never an option. He would continuously tell me how special I was and how he couldn't wait to see me. Traveling over to the UK, I would be treated like royalty. I knew now more than ever that if I made Chanlor official, I would be set for life. Chances like these don't come too often and I wasn't one to past up on an opportunity. After all, life is about risks—high risk, high reward.

As if I didn't have enough on my plate, there is also Seth. Since meeting at the mall we've texted back and forth and talked a couple times, but have yet to go out on a date. To be honest, I can't figure out why I'm actually entertaining him. It's not like his money is long or his conversations are thrilling. He was literally one of those guys that were just something to do, a back-up plan if you will. However, if he doesn't prove himself to be more useful sooner than later, his position on the roster will be swiftly eliminated; I needed contributors, not space fillers.

Since deciding to take my work home for the rest of the week, my schedule became a little more flexible. I was done with all my prospective calls, my presentation for next week's meeting was complete, and my top stocks picks had all experienced gains.

So with my money right and my finances looking prospectively good, it was time to let my hair down and celebrate. Since Karen and I haven't met up in a while, it was imperative that we catch up. I needed to fill her in on everything that was going on, as well as see where things were with her.

After having a glass of wine to kick start the afternoon, I got dressed and headed North on 95 towards downtown Broward. Since Karen landed a gig further north, I figured that Las Olas would be the perfect meeting spot. It was central, popular, and a little more relaxed than the Miami bustle.

Unsure of our exact meeting location, I decided to give Karen a call.

"Hey, boo," answered Karen, energetically.

"Hey, mama," I replied then continued, "Where are you? I think I'm getting close to downtown."

"Well, we'll probably get there at the same time, because I'm exiting as we speak."

"Okay great, so will it be Morton's or Lobster Grille?" I asked.

"Ummm, let's just do Lobster Grille that way we will still be kind of close to the Las Olas area" said Karen before continuing.

"But girl tell me why...."

"Hold on, I have a call coming through; actually I'll just meet you there, let me take this call," I replied cutting Karen off before switching lines.

"Hey, what's going on?" I said the moment I swapped calls.

"Hey sexy, how are you?" replied Seth in a charming tone of voice.

"I'm great, actually, just heading to Broward with a friend of mine for a little late lunch."

"Oh a date, huh; you don't play," he replied with laughter.

"What?"

Chuckling slightly, I continued. "It's actually a girl-friend of mine. We're just meeting up to have a little girl time."

"I'm just messing with you, you know just a little sense of humor. But what I really wanted to do was go out with you later, that's if you have time for me after your girl time and all."

"My schedule is clear afterwards, so yeah, why not we can do something."

"Okay. Well, hit me up when you leave and we'll go from there," said Seth.

"Will do."

After hanging up with Seth I was just moments away from the restaurant. Not wanting to park in a parking garage, I decided to go for what I knew and slid into valet at YOLO. After walking inside briefly, only to visit the bathroom, I walked out and made my way across the street to Lobster Bar.

Although this was one of those spots that lacked a lot of singles, probably due to its more intimate ambience, it was definitely a means to weed out the pheasants and simply relax. Ironically, and to my surprise, as soon as I stepped in the restaurant someone at the bar caught my attention. From a moments glance I could tell that he was a businessman. And from what I could see, he may very well be my type.

In an attempt to get the hostess out of my way in a hurry, I let her know that I was meeting someone there but needed to go to the bathroom first.

As I quickly made my way past the bar and towards the bathroom, I made sure to look in his direction to see if I could make eye contact. Instead he looked down at his phone.

Damn it, I thought.

Not one to slump at a missed opportunity, I decided to continue on to the bathroom, at least that way I would know that my appearance was still on point.

As I entered the bathroom, my phone began ringing. Struggling to find it in my receipt cluttered purse, it continued ringing before finally coming to a stop.

After a couple more seconds of rumbling, I grabbed it as I was immediately taken back by the name of the missed call on the screen.

 It was Mia.

« CHAPTER 10 »

"HEY, MIA, WHAT'S GOING on?" I answered, not sure what to take of her unexpected call.

Since the incident with Mia at the party, she hasn't been answering her phone. If I go to my parent's house, she's either not there or makes attempts to avoid me at all cost. My parents think it's just college jitters that are getting to her, but of course I knew otherwise.

"Hey, how's it going?" she replied in a soft low voice.

"I'm good, is everything okay with you? You don't sound like yourself."

"Yeah, well, I just wanted to talk to you about a few things."

"Go ahead, I can talk," I said.

"Well, not now exactly. I think I'd rather talk to you in person. It's just that...."

She paused.

"Mia, tell me now is everything okay? Are you in any danger?" I pressed.

"No, it's really nothing for you to worry about, I'm fine. Really. I just wanted to talk to you about a couple personal matters that have been bothering me."

"Okay. You know I'm always here to talk; I should be available tomorrow. What I'll do is swing by the house, pick you up, and we can go out for ice cream or something."

"Okay. Just give me a call, I should be home."

Once I hung up the phone I stood in front of the mirror, unable to move. Looking down at the phone, I recalled the conversation in my head a couple of times before I was able to convince myself that she was probably okay.

Figuring that she was finally coming around brought on a blissful feeling that gave me a sense of contentment. I hated the feeling of knowing that my sister was heading down the wrong path and me not being able to stop it.

After finally throwing my phone in my purse, I glanced at myself again in the mirror before trotting out of the bathroom. As I walked towards the bar, I looked in the direction of the guy, only to notice that he was gone.

Great, I thought to myself.

Finally scanning the room for Karen, I could see a hand in the distance, waving away.

"What the hell were you doing in there for so long?" asked Karen as soon as I approached the table.

"I had to powder up, Mom," I replied, smiling as I sat down. "But no, it was Mia, she's finally ready to have a sit down with me, so I told her I would do a something with her tomorrow."

"Yeah, you mentioned what was going on with her, but never got into details."

"Oh boy, where do I start?"

Sitting at the table I filled her in on Mia and her situation, as well as what I had going on with Steven, Chanlor, and Seth.

It was always good talking to Karen because she would give you her unbiased opinion with absolutely no chaser. After hearing all the stories, she was hell bent on me not wasting time with Steven and Seth; it was time to move on to the bigger fish. Agreeing with her slightly, I decided that it would be in my best interest to give Chanlor a little more of my time. The only drawback was the distance—he lived in an entirely different country. But I was willing to make it work because every boss chick knows that once the finances are right, everything else eventfully falls into place.

"So, how are things with you and your new little boo?" I asked.

"Now you know I had to fill you in," replied Karen before continuing, "We are okay; he's just really starting to kind of get on my nerves. It's like every time that I make a move, he wants to be there. If I say I'm going out with friends, the first thing that comes out of his mouth is where and why wasn't he invited."

"What? What guy does that?"

"Oh yeah, it's bad."

"That's not healthy, Karen. You got to watch that kind, he might be a crazed stalker or something."

"I can't deal right now, it's too much. I'm ready to just dismiss his ass and get it over with," replied Karen before continuing, "But anyway, and on some more positive shit, Merlich and I have been getting really close lately. He's actually a nice guy."

"Excuse me! What Merlich? My boss Merlich?"

"Umm, please spare me with the act, Leah; you knew Merlich and I hit it off the night we all went out. Seriously?"

"Oh my God, Karen, I had no idea! I just thought you were drunk and playing nice because he was already there."

"Well, kind of, but then I started looking at him a little differently. We've been talking back and forth and went out a couple of times; I think I like him."

After filling me in more on Merlich, Karen left me in a hazy daze. To put things kindly, I was utterly speechless. Merlich had given me no indication and neither had she.

All in all I was happy for my girl, because I knew the kind of person that Merlich was and I knew what Karen needed. It was no secret at the office how Merlich spoiled his wife and kids with lavish gifts and expensive trips.

After talking a little further, we paid the bill and tipped out of the restaurant. By this point I could definitely feel the alcohol beginning to set in. I felt exhilarated, as if life simply couldn't be better. Everything seemed to be falling back in place. I had a constant flow of cash, Steven at my disposal, Mia appearing to be getting back on track, and now Karen and I would be able to have shopping sprees and trips around the globe. Things were finally beginning to look up.

∞∞∞

After leaving the restaurant, Karen and I said our good-byes before I made my way across the street and back to my car. The night was young and I would definitely not be ending it any time soon. Picking up the phone I called Seth to let him know that I was leaving the downtown area.

As I made my way to the interstate, I was unusually giddy. It was if all the weight that I had been carrying was lifted off in an instant.

Now it was time to see what I had on my hands and what Seth was all about. If he was mediocre in any way, I would have no other choice but to eliminate him. I had no time for mediocrity and no space for time killers. If he wanted to be involved, then he sure as hell had better prove himself or else he would be cut off without even so much of a warning.

Once I pulled up to the address that Seth had given me, I was impressed by his taste in dining. From the looks of it, it appeared to be a very nice restaurant that sat distant from the remaining businesses on the street. The property itself was secluded, with soft warm lights and beautiful floral décor. From the side view I could see an outdoor patio and a stage that stood adjacent to it.

Deciding to apply a little lip gloss before calling Seth, I backed my car into a parking spot and began my mobile glam touch up when out of nowhere I heard a knock on my window. Startled, I dropped the brush insert of the lip gloss directly onto my lap. As I turned to look towards the window, I quickly realized that it was Seth.

"Oh my God, like really? You just scared the hell out of me; this place is too dark and secluded for you to just go around knocking on people's windows like that."

"Dang, I'm sorry, don't kill me. I really didn't mean to scare you—I just didn't want you waiting, thinking that I hadn't made it yet."

"Yeah, but I just got here, so I really wasn't waiting; now I have remnants of lip gloss all over my white jeans," I replied, trying not to sound annoyed.

"Aw man, I'm sorry, sweetie. If you want, I can have that dry cleaned for you," added Seth.

"It's okay, I'll just spray something on it once I get home."

Taking a piece of napkin out of the glove compartment, I dabbed the spot lightly before grabbing my bag and stepping out of the car.

"Looking good," said Seth as he reached out his hand.

After opening the door, we stepped inside the restaurant. Seth immediately gave the host the information about his reservation.

While he was busy talking with the host, I took the extra time to check out the place. The ambience was calming, beautiful, and elegant. In addition to low lighting, there was a waterfall just beside the entrance that gave the atmosphere the relaxing sound of water as the sounds of soft jazz hummed throughout the building.

"Here are some menus for the two of you. Your waiter will be with you shortly," said the host as we were being seated.

Once we placed our drink and subsequently dinner orders, we sipped our drinks slowly, making small talk before the real questions began.

"So, what is it exactly that you do for a living?" I finally managed to ask.

"I am the co-owner of a construction company," replied Seth as he took a sip of his drink.

"Interesting; that seems fun. So how are things with business, considering the recent downturn in the economy?"

"Well, we did take a really harsh hit initially, but it didn't take as long as people think for things to spring back into action."

"Yeah, well it was long enough; luckily I wasn't into the field of finances just yet. But that's the market for ya, highly unpredictable."

As we continued on with dinner, I became more and more impressed with the responses I was receiving. But it was something about his demeanor, something about the way he answered each question. It was if everything was preplanned, and almost too perfect for that matter. Wanting to give him the benefit of the doubt, I decided to take everything he said for face value until he proved otherwise.

"I'll take these out of your way," said the waiter as he reached for our dishes before continuing, "Could I interest the two of you in any desert?"

As I looked over at Seth, we both nodded in agreement that we would pass on any extras.

"I think we're ready for the check," added Seth as he looked at the waiter.

Within minutes the waiter was back with the check, placing it on the table in front of Seth.

Observing his movements I realized that he was looking at the bill a little longer than normal.

"Is everything okay?" I asked curiously.

"Yeah, yeah I was just reading the special offers at the bottom," replied Seth as he eased up in the seat to reach in his back pocket.

After fidgeting through his wallet for another unusual length of time, it became blatantly evident that something was in fact wrong.

"You have got to be kidding me!" added Seth as he continued going through his wallet.

"What's wrong?"

"I grabbed the wrong freaking wallet by accident. I have a work wallet and a leisure wallet that has almost all of my cards."

"This here is my work wallet; how in the hell did I make that mistake—this is so embarrassing," he continued, holding the wallet in the air as he waved it back and forth.

"Oh, wow. I never heard of anyone that has two separate wallets. I can imagine why you got confused."

"I just can't believe that I did that. The only problem now is I don't have enough in this wallet to cover dinner."

As I sat at the table looking squarely in his eyes, I wondered if I had the word 'dunce broad' tatted on my forehead. I cannot believe that a mistaken wallet was the best thing he could come up with—that had to be one of the oldest tricks in a broke man's book. Insulted, I decided to keep my cool and remain a diva. At this point and time, as far as I am concerned, everything that we have established up until to this point was null and void.

"Things happen, don't be so hard on yourself. Give me the check and let me see if I can get with the host; I'll be right back," I replied as I grabbed my bag off the seat of the chair and headed to the front of the restaurant.

"Hey there. I had dinner with the gentleman over there, and what I want to do is pay for my portion of the dinner only."

"Okay, not a problem," said the friendly host."Was everything okay; was the meal to your liking?" He asked.

"Oh no, everything was great. I just have to run, so I'm going to pay for my portion of the bill and I guess he'll handle his once he gets ready to leave."

After handing him my card, he gave me a printed receipt, which I signed before walking out of the door.

Seth was out of his damn mind if he thought he was going to play me into paying for dinner after he offered to take me out. I was born at night, but it definitely wasn't last night. I wish I could be a fly on the wall when he realizes that I'm not there, and his ass has to front his share of the bill. He's lucky that I had a little decency and didn't leave him with the entire check for trying to run such an amateur stunt.

As far as he is concerned, I'm no longer in existence.

Opening the car door I threw my purse on the seat before pulling out my phone, when I noticed several missed calls and texts from Steven. As I previewed the last text, my heart instantly dropped to my knees as chills ran through my body. It read:

I knew I couldn't trust you; you're no different than all the others; that's what I get for trying.

By the way how was dinner?!

« CHAPTER 11 »

AFTER RECEIVING STEVEN'S TEXT, I called him to see exactly what he was talking about, only for the conversation to go nowhere. He continually went on and on about how a friend of his saw me flirting at a restaurant with some unknown male. To kill the conversation and put his mind at ease, I told him that it was just a potential business partner that flew into town and needed to meet before a deal went through.

This was exactly the kind of thing that serves as a distraction from my ultimate goal. It simply was not in my nature to take the necessary time to convince someone of my loyalty. It was time consuming and in the end it was pointless.

To add insult to injury, in the midst of Steven's emotional rant Seth continued calling, repeatedly leaving voicemails on how he couldn't believe I would dip out like that over a minor discrepancy.

Deciding to not respond or entertain his played out games, I simply went to his contact information in my phone and politely blocked him. I owed him nothing, and the audacity of him trying to call me out for counteracting his bum ass move was all the more insulting.

So in an attempt to maintain my current schedule and keep things the way they are, I agreed to meet up with Steven for a sit-down. It was evident that what he witnessed or what was told to him was heavily on his mind, and I just wanted everything to get back on track. Steven seemed like an good guy, if not only for the temporary. I couldn't see myself ruin something beneficial for the loser I just wasted two hours of my life with.

After changing into a pair sweats and a comfy little cami top, I sat on the couch as I awaited Steven's arrival.

In less than five minutes or so I heard the ding of the doorbell.

"Hey, come in," I replied, greeting Steven as I opened the door.

Walking in, he mumbled something that I couldn't understand before making a beeline for the couch.

"Would you like anything to drink or..?" I asked in an attempt to get him to at least say something audible.

"No, I'm fine."

Grabbing a bottle of water for myself, I closed the refrigerator before walking towards the living room where Steven was sitting.

"Okay, so you had a lot to say over the phone and through text, what was that about?

After a short and unusual bream of silence, he cleared his throat before replying. "I said exactly what was told to me, Leah. Someone saw you at some restaurant with some guy. From the way they said you were behaving, it just appeared to me like a little more than a business meeting."

 "You really need to be careful who you listen to, because that's exactly the problem in a lot of relationships today; people listening to other people."

Continuing to sit without saying a word, Steven sat on the couch, staring off at the wall.

"What if I told you that person was me," said Steven as he slowly turned his head towards me.

"Excuse me? So you're following me now?"

"Look, I saw your car leaving downtown Broward and just out of a hunch, decided to follow you. I knew that if you met up with Karen that you probably were drinking and I just wanted to make sure that you made it home safely."

"How convenient; what are the odds? You just happened to be in Broward and spotted me."

"It's the truth, Leah. I care about you and it would kill me to have something happen to you. I know it sounds a little over the top, but I just need to know that I'm not in the blind about anything."

"I have told you everything, Steven. I don't know what else to say, it's your own insecurities that are haunting you."

"Tell me you love me and would never hurt me. I need to know for sure," added Steven as he stood up.

The more I talked to Steven and subsequently dealt with him, the weaker he seemed to be. The aftermath of his parental issues was really coming to a head. Even as an adult, he seemed to be looking for anything to substitute that lost love.

I mean, here is a guy that seemed so well put together; great career, nice car, socially astute, and not to mention seemingly caring, yet he appears to lack the most basic of needs. He needed and demanded love, but unfortunately, I can only guarantee so much. I simply cannot put myself in the position to clean up the mess others left behind; I would essentially be doing myself an injustice.

As I sat on the couch staring into his pitiful eyes, it became clear exactly what he needed. For whatever reason, the desire for physical punishment gave him the sense of fulfillment; I knew exactly how to clear everything up.

With a smile quickly spreading over my face, I rose from the couch and immediately diverted to the bedroom.

Rummaging through the closet, I searched until I found my survivor kit; inside was a pair of black leather boots, a leather shredded whip, and a set of encased hand and leg ties.

Deciding to wear only gloves, a choker, and boots, I stepped out of the room, whip in hand, ready to give him what he has apparently been begging for.

"So, you think it's okay to question and follow me now, huh?" I said as I entered the living room with slow, sway like movements, slashing the whip gently in my hand.

Opening his eyes wide in disbelief, he stood by the sofa speechless as his eyes began traveling up and down my body.

"Take off all of your fucking clothes right now; you have less than a minute," I added assertively while continuing to tap the whip in my hand.

Like a schoolboy under command, Steven immediately began taking off his shoes in a hasty rush, as if his life depended on it. Within moments he was standing in front of me, hands by his side and completely naked.

"So, I have a few house rules that I need you follow. Whenever I ask you a question, you are required to answer it quickly and it must always end with the statement 'yes, your highness.' Likewise, whenever I tell you to do something, you must continue to do it until I give you the command to stop. I also need you to understand that during this state you are considered property and whatever I ask of you should never be questioned. Do I make myself clear?"

"Yes, your highness," replied Steven, continuing to gaze at me with a wild look in his eyes.

"Now drop to your knees and lick my boots until I tell you otherwise."

Like a pleasing servant, he fell to his knees and began licking my boots as if he were a cat drinking milk.

About a minute later I ordered him to stop. "Get your pitiful ass up, and hurry up," I shouted, slashing him across the back with the whip.

Jumping up immediately, he stood in front of me with his hands by his sides, showing no emotion.

Circling around him, I spat on him several times to signify my disrespect and inherent sexual power. Kneeling on the couch, I began spreading my legs as I tooted my ass up in the air.

"Bring your ass over here and suck on this pussy until I tell you to stop. When I yell 'switch,' I need you to immediately start licking my ass."

As Steven approached me, I turned around and whipped him as hard as I could from his left thigh all the way up to his arm. Staring at him in disgust and anger, I began tapping his penis lightly as I watched for a change in his facial expression. As his face began to knit up in apparent pain, a devilish grin spread widely over my face.

"Didn't I tell you how to respond to each request? Don't let me have to tell you to say 'yes, your highness' again, do you hear me?" I added through clinched teeth.

"Yes, your highness," he quickly responded.

"Now be a good servant and follow through with your duties, and don't let your measly filthy paws come in contact with me," I continued, turning around as I resumed my position on the couch.

"Yes, your highness."

Like the obedient servant, Steven dropped to his knees and began softly sucking on my clitoris. The scene, the mastery power and the feeling of my clit being manipulated, was more than I could mentally phantom. After what felt like seconds, my body began to shake as the feeling of fluid shot out of my body.

"Stick your tongue inside of me and catch every drop of this cum; and don't you dare waste a bit of it!" I demanded through exasperated breaths.

As he followed my command, the effects of my constant tightening muscles seem to be more than I could bear. Grinding on his tongue I began to scream in ecstasy, holding my breath as I uncontrollably began to squirt yet again. After feeling my body calm to almost a bare limp, I yelled for him to switch, which he did without hesitation.

The recurrent warm, wet strokes of his tongue along the inside of my ass was all the more pleasing. With my mouth wide open and my eyes closed shut, I exasperated with short, shallow breaths as I welcomed the orgasmic feeling. Turning around quickly, I ordered him to go and retrieve the facial strap-on that I had left in my closet. Spreading out on the couch, I gently began rubbing my clitoris as I awaited his return.

"Strap it on and do your duties!" I commanded the moment he re-entered the room.

"Yes, your highness."

After putting it on and adjusting it to his head, he bent down and slowly began circling the rim of my vagina, veering deeper and deeper with each gentle push.

"Good boy. Keep doing it just like that."

"You were made for this, you're such a good servant. If you keep this up, you're going to earn your doggy treats quicker than I thought."

Looking up at me with droopy yet pleasing eyes and without saying a word signified his gratitude and unswaying commitment.

∞∞∞

The first half of the next day seemed to be a blurry haze. After last night's events, my body screamed and demanded that I rest. With such a long break from drama, men, and partying, I would definitely have to get used to the demands of my newly created lifestyle. It seems like just when I think things are slowing to calm, something unexpected happens and everything is back into a tailspin.

Luckily, last night's escapade seem to put Steven in better spirits. Having slept over, he woke up early, made breakfast, and served me in bed; it was as if the restaurant incident never happened. Just like that, I was forgiven for something that deep inside he probably knew was a lie. It's funny how life can sometimes flip the script, and while I don't blame Steven for my distrust in men, he undoubtedly is footing the bill from some of my past suitors.

But on the flip side, I was ready for him to leave the moment I woke up. Not only was he blocking me from answering Chanlor's calls, but I also didn't want him to get used to the idea of sleeping over. He still needed to be taught that spending the night would not be regarded as commonplace, but as a generous gesture redeemable only by invite.

Flipping around in bed once Steven left, I decided to finally get up and get my day started before I ended up sleeping it away. I managed to text Mia about today's meet up, and she agreed for me to pick her up around three. Though tired, I was excited; it's been a while since Mia had been her old self. And like the overprotective big sis, I would give anything to see that cute little smile yet again.

The very moment I decided to drag myself out of bed, my phone began ringing. Looking over at the screen, I realized it was Chanlor. Almost immediately I began clearing the morning harshness from my throat before answering.

"Hey, babe," I answered in a soft angelic monotone.

"Darling, how are you? You had me worried there for a bit when I couldn't get through to you," replied Chanlor in his sexy British accent.

"I knooow. I didn't realize that my phone was on silent, I was so upset when I woke up and realized that I had missed all of your calls."

"Well, perhaps it's where you're waking up that's the problem."

"I totally agree," I replied, feeling flattered.

"I tell you what, take some time off from work and fly here. I can have one of my assistants book you a flight as early as today, or I could have one of my pilots there as soon as tomorrow.

Speechless, I stood quiet before responding. "I mean, yeah, why not, that would be great. But I don't think today or tomorrow will be possible, sweetie; that's just too short notice for me."

 "Very well, I have a little patience. Check out your schedule, forward me the dates and then we can go from there."

"Okay, I'll definitely jump on top of that. I know for sure that I have an important presentation that's coming up soon that I have to prepare for and attend, but after that I'm pretty much open."

"Is this for work?" he asked.

"Yes."

"Darling, what they're paying you is minuscule to what I can provide for you. Going to a crummy job should be the least of your present concerns, but if you wish, I will remain patient and give you some time to get the ball rolling; just don't have me waiting too long, or then I'll have to come and find you."

Blushing, I gleefully comforted him by giving him my promise. It was clearer than ever that Chanlor was a man with power that was used to getting his way. He had a boss-like calmness that would make an enemy want to join his team.

No longer tired and now gleaming with excitement, I envisioned my trip to the UK: the shopping sprees, exquisite dining, and explorations was just what I needed. It was time that I ventured outside of these Miami streets to see what the rest of the world had to offer.

 Some may call it gold digging, but for me it was business. Business done internationally.

«Chapter 12»

"Thanks for picking me up. These three days without a car has been driving me insane," grunted Mia as she got in the car.

"I can only imagine; not to mention the inconvenience of waiting on Mom and Dad to go places," I replied as I backed out my parent's driveway.

"Please don't mention it."

"But anyway, what's been going on with you?

"Oh God, Leah, I don't know; it's like things just changed overnight."

"What do you mean? With who?"

"With Justin. And before you go on your 'I told you so' rant, just hear me out for a second."

From the moment I heard the name Justin, my stomach felt like it had balled up in a knot. Sadly, I knew this moment would be coming sooner than later.

"No, not at all, go on. I'm not here to judge."

"Okay, well things were going great with us until the night of the party. Like, right after you guys left, we decided to stay and continue chilling. After maybe an hour or so, Justin pulled me to the side saying something to the effect of him having an idea that could make us some money. So of course I questioned him on what it was, do you know that this SOB had the nerve to say that we could set one of the guys up from the party and rob them? His plan for me was to lure the guys in by masturbating for them at the party house and then promising each of them more at a different location."

"Stop it right there! I don't even want to hear anymore," I interjected, throwing my hand in the air as I cut her off. "What kind of man solicits his supposed to be girlfriend as a means for quick cash? I mean, I've seen a couple dirt bags, but never in my life have I ever heard of this. I'm really trying not to hit you with the 'I told you so line,' but Mia, you've really got to trust the people who genuinely care for you a little more. A lot of times when you're in a relationship you get so wrapped up with the person that you really don't see the bigger picture; but others can. Just remember that nothing I say or do is done with malicious intent. I saw the looks on that idiot's face and I knew that his intentions weren't loyal; which is exactly the reason I kept reaching out to you after the party."

"Speaking of looks," added Mia before continuing.

"That was another thing that bothered me. He had this crazy way of staring at you that I told him I didn't like. But what got my attention the most was the fact that he was always asking questions about you."

"What the hell does he need to know about me?"

"Just questions, like things he shouldn't need the answer to. It kind of made me feel like he had some kind of interest in you. And please don't be mad at me, but that's kind of what made me so angry with you. I just didn't want the first guy that I really liked to slip away from me; especially for my sister."

"Mia, I would never do something like that to you. It doesn't matter who or what, we're sisters; family!"

The more I talked to my sister, the more I was convinced that this was just part of her growing up. Although I wanted to shield her as much as I could, some lessons are just better learned through experience.

Although it was a very bad situation and could have progressively been worse, I'm just happy having my sister back. Just like old times we talked, shopped, ate ice cream, and clowned around till late evening going into the night. Mia evened managed to reunite with a really cute guy that she knew in middle school, someone her own age.

After grabbing a bite to eat, we decided that it was time to head home and call it a day.

"Aw man, it was a relief to get out of the house and do something different, something legal," said Mia, giggling.

"Yeah, I enjoyed you as well pumpkin—you know you're one of my favorite people in the whole wide world," I added, playfully pinching her cheeks. But one more thing: please, please, please promise me that it's over for sure. You cannot let yourself be a victim of this type of guy or anyone else like him. He's a pimp and uses women for his own financial gain."

"I promise," replied Mia, stopping briefly when my phone started to ring.

"Hey, sweetie," I said, answering the phone.

"Hey, you. I guess you've been busy; I haven't heard from you all day," replied Steven.

"Yeah, I've just been out with Mia doing a little shopping and bonding. What are you up to?"

"Mia, huh? Don't try to use your sister as a scapegoat for your wrong doings."

"Excuse me? Doings?" I replied, before continuing, "Look, Steven, don't even start. I thought we were past that stage. That was one isolated incident and I told you exactly what it was all about."

Looking over at Mia, I shook my head as I rolled my eyes, causing her to giggle.

"Relax, babe, I was only kidding around with you. Why are you so uptight?" added Steven.

Deciding not to get into a confrontation with him, I quickly changed the subject. At this point I'm beginning to contemplate on whether sexual domination was going to be enough to keep him in check. Was this a watered down attempt to get my attention?

I was never the type of female to argue or constantly debate with any one person—and I damn sure wasn't about to start. I couldn't make money from arguing and I couldn't focus on getting things in order if I spent all my time arguing, especially to a middle class man with childhood issues.

After small talking with Steven for a little bit longer, I ended the call by telling him that I had to get a few things in order with Mia before dropping her off. Reluctantly agreeing, I assured him that I would call once I left my parent's house.

As soon as I ended the call, the answers to my questions were no longer of concern. It was evident that Steven was not going to last much longer on my roster. His attempted control over me, and my whereabouts, was without question unacceptable.

Deciding to let him down cautiously, I preplanned my next move. I would either tell him outright or just avoid him all together. Either way, the jury has come to a unanimous decision: Steven's position was up for elimination.

∞∞∞

The rest of the weekend and the first part of the next week went without a hitch. I was back on schedule with my clients and I managed to score a huge deal that rewarded me nicely with a hefty bonus. I just recently got my anniversary raise, my top stock picks were outperforming their counterparts, and Chanlor did not hesitate to bless me regularly.

Since my decision to eliminate Steven over the weekend, we haven't talked much, let alone seen each other. Whenever he called I would quickly tell him that I was busy. If I did manage to talk to him, the conversation didn't last past five minutes.

Finally questioning my recent unavailability, I quickly blew it off on a hectic schedule and didn't elaborate much further. Hoping that he would eventually get the picture and end up finding someone else, I felt content and confident in my final decision to carry out the break-up. Apart from his insecurities, he would make a great husband; just not for me. I've never been into the construction business; time for me was my greatest asset, and like anything else it would take time to construct the perfect man.

Unfortunately for me, Chanlor had to leave the UK abruptly and head to South America on business. Not being able to give me an exact return date, he assured me that he would keep in contact while he was there. According to him, he was offered a business deal he simply couldn't refuse.

Hesitating to ask him his exact means of business, I shuffled around the question only to get vague and somewhat general answers. Though eagerly curious, at the end of the day it really didn't matter. It was evident that he was a man of great wealth and exceeding power, and maybe this is exactly what has me so intrigued. It was just something about a man that took control and could make money at the drop of a dime that moistened my G-strings; that shit was sexy. To add even more fire to the flame was our chemistry, added with his conservative appearance and bad boy swag that undoubtedly gave him the leading edge.

As I sat at my desk going through emails and reminiscing about Chanlor, I was interrupted suddenly by a knock on my office door.

"Come in," I yelled out.

"Hey, hard worker, how's it going?" asked Merlich as he entered.

"It's going, just reviewing a few accounts for the upcoming week."

"Great. Before I go on, I just want to commend you on all of your hard work. You are the youngest and most recent executive, yet you have outperformed all of the senior executives two quarters in a row; that is truly commendable."

"Thank you, thank you, thank, you. It is equally rewarding to be with a leading company that is able to help me bring out my true abilities; I couldn't be happier."

"You're made for this, girl," he playfully replied. "But another thing I wanted to come over and talk to you about is the training seminar that's going to be held in New York this year. I believe that this particular one is going to be a week long and will be at a conference center in upper Manhattan. This one is going to be very informational and I'm planning on clearing my schedule just to attend it. I was wondering if you wanted to attend it as well. Oh, and just veering off topic slightly, I know your girl filled you in on what we decided on," added Merlich.

"Who? Karen?" I asked curiously.

Waving his hand in the air he made motions for me to lower my voice as he shook his head in agreement.

"Yes, I invited her to come along," he whispered before continuing, "I figured if she came along as an extra person, we could all turn the trip into a personal one after each conference."

"Well, that sounds fun. Why not?" I answered happily.

"Great. I'll send you the details in an email. Remember to contact Jenny to go over your flight details and spending allowance," he quickly added before walking out of the office.

As soon as he closed the door, I couldn't wait to get on the phone and slaughter Karen for keeping the news.

"Hey, lil mama," answered Karen.

"'Hey lil mama,' my ass. I just called to hear about this trip you and you know who are planning on taking."

Karen immediately broke in laughter before replying. "You know what, I really, really wanted to tell you, but I got so tied up with my job and everything else; besides, he wanted to run everything by you first."

"Well that's not what he said, he thought I knew! Besides, you know I would have still acted surprised if push came to shove."

Giggling slightly she continued. "Now, Leah, you've known me for far too long. You know I wouldn't have kept something like that from you; it really just slipped my mind. But on another note, I must say that I'm really feeling this Merlich guy. Girl, since meeting him, my rent has been paid up for months and my pockets stay lined. He's kind of the deal for me right now.

"Well damn, I didn't think things were that deep, considering the other situation; you know what I mean," I replied, making sure to talk as low as possible.

"Please! I don't care about that; I'm comfortable with the fact that he has a wife. It actually makes things better for me—I don't have to worry about holding down the household and carrying all the weight. I get what I want, he gets someone who is fun and vibrant, so really it works perfectly—in the end we're both happy."

"I hear ya. I know if no one else can play the game, you sure as hell can. So by all means, do what you think is best for you."

"But what happened to dude that had you tied down all this time?"

"He's around, but that lock down shit is a thing of the past. I can't lie, he tried, but when I found out that his ass was full of lies and not to mention broke—I cut that short real quick."

After talking further with Karen, I was forced to end the call due to a mandatory executive meeting. It was always refreshing to chitchat with my girl. It was also refreshing to see her happy and her financial situation looking a little more positive.

So with Chanlor's blooming money tree and Merlich's non-stop cash, Karen and I had the opportunity to become very wealthy women. We were ole G's in the game and knew whole-heartedly that a man was not a long-term financial plan. So until we got to the point where we could hold it down lavishly on our own, piggybacking off them for now simply had to do.

Feeling exhilarated and exceedingly confident, I gathered my presentation notes and read over them briefly before leaving my office.

Entering the conference room, I realized that a few people were apparently late since a couple of chairs sat empty. Not even Merlich, who was known to be prompt, had made to the meeting.

Grabbing a seat closer to the edge of the table, I began mentally preparing myself for what I would say, when Merlich's secretary, Jenny, suddenly interrupted my thoughts.

"I really hope that this meeting isn't long and drawn out, my son's soccer game starts in an hour and I need to be there," whispered Jenny.

"Yeah, I hope so to, but it's not looking good; think about it we're already off to a late start."

Continuing to talk she went on and on about her son, husband, and anything else that seemed to pop in her head. Looking on, I continued to sit there, as if I was interested in her blabbering and boring personal life. Getting annoyed, I searched for a means of diverting my attention.

"Excuse me for a sec, I need to run back to my office for minute. I think I left my phone," I said as I pushed my chair back and stood up.

The moment I opened my office door, I immediately heard the distinctive sound of a notification coming in. Grabbing the phone from my desk, I realized that it was a text from Karen. As I began reading the preview of the text, I was taken aback. Curious as to what it was regarding, I immediately entered my pass code and went straight to her message.

> *I really want to ask you something but I don't want to rub you the wrong way or make you feel uncomfortable. As you know, we have been friends for years and I would never try to intentionally disrespect you or put you in harm's way, but I*

really need your assistance in carrying something out. I was wondering if you would be open to having a little fun with the Mister and me. Before you shoot down the idea, please think about it....

« CHAPTER 13 »

IN THE DAYS FOLLOWING KAREN'S message, I made the conscious effort to neither respond to it nor contact her. Initially, I was taken aback and sort of felt weird about the whole situation. Karen was like a sister to me and I didn't want to put our friendship through any unnecessary tribulations. Needless to say, Merlich was my boss and I knew that it was never a good idea to mix business with pleasure; especially when it was relative to my well-being.

The more I thought about it, the more I became convinced that Merlich had put her up to it. It just wasn't Karen's style to make sexual advances, especially to other women. I know people say that you never really know a person, but I consider myself to be an excellent judge of character, and in this situation there was definitely a deeper issue than what was on the surface.

In an attempt to clear my mind and get a different perspective on everything that was going on, I decided to make plans with Jasmine and possibly hit up the nail shop for a little girl time. It's been a while since we've hung out and, quite honestly, she may be just the person to talk to about Karen, and not to mention Steven. Maybe she can help me unveil the reason for "friendship" hook-ups and the reason behind Steven's sudden erratic behavior.

Was it something about me that made me an object of sexuality? Was my personality that laid back that people felt comfortable approaching me with their ill demands of gratification? As I pondered over these thoughts, I tried to dissect their overall reasoning when my phone suddenly began ringing. Peering at the screen, I saw that it was Karen.

"Hey," I answered, bracing myself for the unknown.

"Hey you, what's going on?"

"Just home relaxing for the moment, I'm supposed to be going out with Jasmine in an hour or so though. What's good?"

"Okay, cool. What's going on with her? I didn't think you guys still hung out."

"Well, she called the other day and was complaining about issues she was having with some guy she was dating—I think she just needs someone to talk to."

"Oh gosh, it's always something with these dudes, I tell ya. Did I tell you about what buddy tried with me?" added Karen.

"No. What happened?" I asked nervously, afraid of what her next words could be.

"He had the freaking nerve to ask me if he could move in until he gets things back rolling."

"Ohhhh, that buddy. Wow, really?" I replied, secretly relieved.

As the conversation continued, my guards slowly fell. We spent the next forty-five minutes discussing everything under the sun. It was as if the text never happened.

Either way I was relieved. Maybe not responding was actually a good thing. Though her failure to mention it does seem rather odd, I'm happy that the awkward feeling won't have to linger around for an eternity. Maybe things will just move forward and the advance will simply be a faded memory; something to laugh about later.

Deciding to not think further on the topic, I figured it was time that I got dressed and prepared to head out. Knowing that I would be late, I sent Jasmine a text that I was running behind and not to rush. Replying that she was experiencing the same, we agreed to meet at the new nail bar near my house.

The moment I walked back into the bedroom and pulled off my robe, my phone began ringing yet again. Looking at the ID, I realized that it was Steven.

"Oh gosh, here we go again," I said aloud as I silenced the call.

His complaining and clinginess were beginning to annoy me. Even if I decided to silence him by feeding into his deviant desires, the silence would only be temporary and by tomorrow we would be back to our regularly scheduled programming. So, instead of playing by his rules, I decided to simply not answer any of his calls until I was ready to talk.

Immediately dismissing the thought, I turned on my Pandora, opened up the blinds, and proceeded to get dressed. The first song that popped on was *Let's Chill* by the group Guy. Turning on my surround sound, I was immediately ensnared by the rhythm as I imagined my trip to see Chanlor. Creating the scene in my head, I could just feel him grabbing me tightly in his arms, smiling giddily as I entered my chauffeured ride. It would be nothing short of magical; the two of us meeting up yet again, only this time on a deeper level.

The more Chanlor and I talked, the deeper things were becoming. It was as if we knew each other in a past life or something; it was just that close of a connection.

Carrying on with my happy thoughts, I showered, got dressed, and lightly powdered my face. With the humidity and my already smooth complexion, there was no need for a full face of makeup. In fact, most people felt like I looked better without it. And although I would never step out without at least loose powder, it was refreshing to know that my natural beauty outshone my best painted routine.

Once I was done admiring myself in the mirror, I splashed on some D&G Cool Blue before examining my attire in the full body mirror down the hall. It was imperative that I was always on point. Other than Chanlor, my list had practically dried up. I needed excitement, something new and adventurous; someone other than Steven to keep me entertained.

∞∞∞

"You look nice," said Jasmine as she walked up to hug me.

"Thank you, and I love that dress, it looks so summery and comfortable on you," I replied through our embrace before continuing, "Did you get a new car?"

"Not yet. I'm driving my dad's car for now, at least until I can save up a little more cash and cop my own."

"Oh okay, you know I was just wondering because I was kind of expecting for you to ask me to pick you up."

The truth of the matter is that I was just being nosey, and wanted to see if she had dropped a new whip. In the three years Charles has been gone, it has been all the more apparent that she relied heavily on whatever he was giving her—obviously never stopping to seek out her own.

When will these girls ever learn, I thought to myself.

"So, how have you been?" asked Jasmine, interrupting my thoughts.

"I can't complain. How about yourself? It's been awhile since we last saw each other; since that last party, right?"

"I believe so. Dang, it really has been a while, hasn't it?" she replied.

As we walked towards the nail bar, she went on to tell me about her new job and new perspective on life. She was dating again and things were apparently looking up for her.

Once we received two glasses of wine and were seated for our pedicures, she went on to discuss the drama that she was going through with a few family members. Like always, Jasmine seemed to have the ability to go from story to story before you could even get a chance to comment on the one before. I was now convinced that she could not possibly have any other friends to talk to; at least any that cared to hear her problems. Either way, I was not going to have the entire day be focused on her and her petty problems; there were bigger things going on that we needed to discuss.

As she stopped briefly to talk with the pedicurist, I took advantage of the opportunity and quickly switched gears.

"So Jasmine, what is really going on with your boy Steven?"

"What do you mean?" she asked as she knitted up her forehead, appearing to be taken off guard by the question.

Taking a sip of my wine I continued. "What I mean by that is, he's been acting kind of strange lately. Long story short, I've been kind of busy lately with work and what-not, so I really haven't been seeing much of him. I'm guessing because of this, he feels the need to question my whereabouts and even going as far as to saying someone saw me somewhere with a guy; I mean like really getting upset about it."

Pausing slightly I continued. "Just within the short span of time we've known each other, Steven has become more and more controlling and kind of needy; it's like he wants my attention twenty-four-seven."

Peering over my glass slightly to catch any unusual facial expressions, I continued sipping as I waited for her input on the topic.

After taking one foot out of the water and placing it on the chairs pedestal, she breathed a sigh before finally speaking.

"Leah, I really didn't want to get into this. I mean, I'm just not one to get into people's business. But I have heard these same allegations once before."

Adjusting myself in the chair, I looked onward as I waited for her to continue. Clasping her hands tightly in an indirect praying motion, she brought them down slowly before continuing.

"Go on," I egged. "With who and what happened?"

"Well, this happened like five years ago, around the same time I met Charles, actually. Steven at the time was dating this one chick and things seemed to be going great with them, until one day when I got a call from Charles saying that Steven had spazzed and was talking crazy. No one knew what was wrong with him, so they eventually had to admit him to Jackson. Word on the street was that Steven had taken a concoction of drugs and it made him go crazy. He was going around saying that people were out to get him because of things that he apparently knew. Every time that I would see him, he was always literally looking over his shoulder, insisting that he was being followed. Oh my God, this is bringing up old memories that I wanted to keep buried," she added while rubbing her eyes.

"Wait a minute, you mean to tell me Charles and Steven are buddies? And Steven is a labeled nut?"

"Well, not buddies, but they did apparently know each other in college, and through passing, I guess."

What are the freaking odds, I thought to myself.

I desperately wanted her to go on, but the unmistakable feeling of anger was slowly brewing inside of me. Why in the hell did she act as if it was okay for me to date someone like this? When I asked her about him initially, why was this not brought up?

It was quickly becoming apparent that Jasmine was not the cool person she was portraying herself to be. I knew all along that it was just something about her; I just couldn't put my finger on it. Why didn't I just wean myself away from her before I got myself into unnecessary, idiotic drama?

Interrupting my thoughts, she continued. "He ended up spending three months there before he was released. But once he was out, he completely changed his life; even the people he hung out with. He got a new, higher paying job and seemed to be adjusting well until questions start arising about the girl that he was dating."

"What questions?" I asked eagerly as my nerves began to flutter.

"Questions on her whereabouts," she replied before continuing, "From what I heard about the case, her family reported her missing just days after Steven went to Jackson. When her mom couldn't get a hold of her, she filed a missing person report with the Miami-Dade police. They investigated her whereabouts and interviewed a long list of people who apparently had dealings with her, including Steven. No one could give account as to where she could possibly be; the whole situation was just crazy, man."

As I sat there, it took everything in me to not reach over and grab her. No friend of mine, or even close associate, would have ever allowed me to date someone who apparently had a case of suspected mental illness. Was this her insidious way of getting back at me over Charles?

Regardless of her intentions or the final outcome, this was officially it. Once I got all the information that I needed, her ass is officially blocked; no questions asked. There was no way in hell that I would allow myself to continue to fro lock around with the devil.

"So where was she?" I asked, this time in an angrier tone of voice.

Sighing heavily, she shook her head as she twisted her lips to the side. "Good question," she went on to say. "For all I know, she's still considered a missing person."

"Still considered a missing person! What do you mean 'still considered a missing person?'" I yelled out causing everyone in the salon to get quiet.

Disregarding the stares I continued. "So, what you're telling me is that you had prior knowledge on someone who apparently has a mental condition and was admitted to a mental hospital, whose girlfriend at the time went missing and is still missing to this day. And not once did it occur to you that this was information worth sharing?"

"Leah, please, I..."

Taking my feet out of the glass bowl while slowly rising from my seat, I continued cutting her off.

Let me tell you something, I don't give a damn what you and Charles had going on. He lied to the both of us, but for you to stoop this fucking low is baffling!"

"Leah, just hear me out for one second, please. This has nothing to do with Charles. Like I told you before, Steven is a friend of the family, and what I knew about him, he just didn't seem capable of doing something like that."

"I'm sorry, -- too much noise. We can't have the noise here," said Jasmine's nail tech in broken chopped up English.

Dismissing her nail techs' comment I continued.

"Excuse me? So you're the judge and the jury now. Just when did you have the qualifications to determine who did what?" I replied to Jasmine angrily.

After drying off my toes with a nearby towel, I grabbed my purse and threw it across my arms.

"Your ass is just as crazy as he is," I added before handing my nail tech a twenty-dollar bill for starting my pedicure.

"Leah, wait," yelled Jasmine as I walked out of the shop.

Deciding to speak no further, I continued walking through the door as I headed straight for the car. As I walked, a whirlwind of emotions swirled throughout my head. With everything that's going on, I don't even know who's left to trust.

Driving home, I tried gravely to put together the pieces of the puzzle and make sense of it all. Who were these people that I had let into my life? Deep inside, I had known that Jasmine was not to be trusted, but I would have never imagined that things were as deep as they were with Steven. Cutting Jasmine off was no biggie, but how would I get away from Steven? He seemed overly obsessed, and to make matters worse, knew where I lived. What if he really did have something to do with his ex's disappearance?

As the thoughts and questions continued circling throughout my mind, I pondered on how I could end things with Steven without putting my life in jeopardy.

Having no real resolve, I began tapping the steering wheel furiously with my thumb when I suddenly realized that I had already made it home. Pulling into my parking space, I peered around the area to see if anyone was lurking. Noticing nothing out of the norm, I grabbed the door handle and immediately hopped out of the car.

Racing up the walkway, I continued looking back as I was now overcome with fear. Finally making it to my doorway, I quickly pushed the key in the door, opened it slightly, and quickly slipped in. The sound of the door shutting and the lock turning gave me the overall sense of security. I was safe from the harm and all the dangers of the world.

Placing my bag on the counter, I headed straight for the wine rack and grabbed an unopened bottle of merlot. Retrieving a glass from the cupboard, I filled the glass to the top before making my way to my bedroom.

It was only six o'clock in the evening and I was practically beat! My body felt as though I had worked and eighteen-hour shift. I was stressed, angry, and fearful of the future. With so many mixed emotions, the overbearing feeling of just going to sleep and forgetting it all started to nag at me. But although my mind wanted to rest, my body felt stiff and tense.

Lying on the bed and staring up at the ceiling, I began to feel the nagging sensation of a feeling that was all too familiar during times of undue stress. Acting on my emotions, I pulled down my pants and slipped off my panties.

Closing my eyes, I licked my finger as I began rubbing the top of my clitoris. Starting in gentle circular motions, I continued rubbing myself systematically until I began feeling more and more wetness. Proceeding downward, I slide my fingers inside, gliding them slowly back and forth.

The feeling of relief was just what I needed. As I continued to get more and more heated, I reached towards my nightstand in search of my little pink bunny. Opening my eyes slightly, I quickly switched it on. The sound and feel of the vibration created a static-like feeling that radiated throughout my entire body. Slipping my finger through the ring of the bunny I immediately began tapping my pussy gently, as the catalyzed motions caused a sudden stream of fluid to shoot across the room.

Breathing heavily, I could feel my body physically tighten, as I uncontrollably began to squirm in wave-like motions. Subconsciously anticipating what was to come, my breaths intensified as my body temperature began to rise.

Suddenly my phone began to ring. Slightly thrown off track, I closed my eyes as I made attempts to tune out the external distraction. Continuing to rub myself, I waited patiently for the ringing to stop.

Within of second or so of stopping, the ringing started once again. Annoyed, I jumped off the bed to see what was the emergency. The moment my feet touched the floor, repeated pounding on the front door instantly startled me.

Standing still, I froze in indescribable horror. As the pounding continued, I gazed around the room franticly in search for my phone. Seeing it on the dresser, I grabbed my pants as I tiptoed in its direction.

Stopping only for a moment, the pounding continued on like an orchestrated cadence. Creeping silently towards the door, I peered through the peephole only to confirm my worst fear. Standing there with a crazed and erratic look was Steven.

« CHAPTER 14 »

"OPEN THE DOOR, LEAH. I can see you at the peephole," said Steven in an unusual. yet desperate, tone of voice after knocking and pounding repeatedly.

Backing up slightly, I made every attempt to remain silent as I slowly slipped my pants back on.

"Leah, open the damn door; I'm not leaving here until I talk to you. I really just want to talk to you."

"Steven, you need to leave before I call the cops," I yelled while fearfully looking at the door.

"Call the cops? Call the cops on me? What the hell did I do to you for you to want to call the cops!" he replied loudly.

"What is it that you want to talk about? I can hear you loud and clear through the door," I quickly added before the sounds of a loud thud shook the door.

My heart rate began to increase as I realized the origin of the sound was Steven, apparently trying to break down the door.

"Look, if you're going to act animalistic and try to beat down the door, then you leave me no choice but to call in on you. So I suggest that you calm down if you want me to as much as respond to you right now," I yelled in a strong and stern tone of voice.

"Okay, okay. I'm sorry. It's just that I really want to talk to you about some things. But I really can't do it from this side of the door. Just let me in for a few minutes; I promise once I say what I have to say, if you don't want to talk to me anymore I'll leave."

Oh yeah, he's definitely crazy, I thought to myself.

"No, the way you approached the door said it all, there is no way I'm letting you in here."

"God damn it, Leah!" yelled Steven before he was interrupted by a set of strange voices.

Edging closer to the edge of the door, I held my breath as I poked my head forward to get a better listening spot. It quickly became clear that someone must have called the cops. I could overhear them asking him did he live in the area and why was he here disturbing the neighborhood. As I tried to make out what he was saying, I could hear one of the cops directing him away from the door and out to the parking lot.

Still visibly shaken, I breathed a long sigh of relief that at least someone was here to quell the situation. This was definitely one of those instances that could have ended very badly. How did I get myself involved with someone like this? If only I could turn back the hands of time, I would have kept it moving and gone about my business. If only I had met Chanlor sooner, I probably wouldn't have even given this undercover nutcase the time of day.

The more I stood there and pitted the situation, the more freighted I became. Still in utter shock, I was unsure on whether to run, cry, or fight back somehow. My mind, for the first time, was in a blank, dark place.

∞∞∞

Slowly opening my eyes, I could see the sun shining brightly through the openings of the blinds. When suddenly, as if someone hit a light switch, the feeling of nervousness came over me. Hesitating only briefly, I snatched back the sheets as I looked down to see what I was wearing. My distressed jeans and fitted tee confirmed the ugly truth. What happened last night was indeed a reality.

Rising out of bed, I rubbed my eyes as I tried to collect my thoughts. As objects slowly became clearer, the first thing that caught my eye was a yellow carbon copy document, along with miscellaneous other papers spread out across my nightstand. Veering closer, I realized that it was the police report from last night along with a number of other victim's rights brochures.

As much as I wanted it to just be a horrible nightmare, I could no longer deny the truth. The acceptance of this reality brought the events of last night rushing back through my mind.

After talking with Steven, the police came in and got my side of the story. I relayed to them our history and what possibly brought on his apparent anger. Unbeknownst to me at the time, Steven had apparently become belligerent and attempted to break free of the handcuffs that were placed on him while repeatedly continuing to yell.

With my written statement and his blatant acts of violence, he was placed under arrest and taken to the county jail, where he awaits medical attention.

Hidden amongst the scattered paperwork was a temporary restraining order that barred Steven from contacting me by phone or in person. As I stared at the paper, I knew that things for me had officially changed. Everything that Jasmine had relayed to me just hours ago was quickly coming to fruition. It was as if she predicted the future, only I had survived a potentially dangerous guy, at least for now, before he was able to carry out any of his heinous acts of violence.

Still revving from the events from the night before, I tried desperately to keep my thoughts focused on the positive aspect of things. Knowing that he would be incarcerated for at least a day, I knew that I only had a limited amount of time to plan my next move.

There was no way that I would continue staying here alone, alarm or no alarm. It was evident that Steven had no boundaries; even the presence of the police couldn't even alter his volcanic behavior.

Deciding to call Chanlor in an attempt to clear my mind, I picked up the phone and dialed his number.

"Hello, sweetheart, there's that voice that I've been dying to hear. How are you?" he asked.

"Hey, baby, I'm great, just needed to hear your voice as well."

Chanlor and I continued to talk about his trip, and the trip that we were planning. I tried to talk to him as normal as possible so that he would have no indication that anything that was happening out of the ordinary. I didn't want to risk losing someone like Chanlor because I was fro locking around with a mediocre lunatic. I had to keep this secret just that, a secret.

After hanging up with Chanlor, I decided to fill Karen in on everything that took place. Shocked and equally afraid, she suggested that I crash over her place until things blew over. In agreement, I gathered all the things that I thought I would need for the week and packed them before heading out. Although Karen was my girl and I knew that she didn't mind me crashing over, I would without question be uncomfortable with it being such an extended amount of time. Like any other girl, I needed my space and privacy. Not to mention Karen's recent unusual advances.

This should be interesting, I thought to myself.

Pulling my bags out of the house, I decided that my first stop would indeed be by my parents and then Karen's.

Never a dull moment in my world, I thought inwardly as I threw my bags in the trunk. *Never a dull moment.*

Speeding out the driveway, the only thing that was left on my mind was to place as much distance as possible to any places that Steven knew I would be. Aside from work, he would definitely have a hard time finding me.

The entire drive to my parent's house was a complete blur. Before even realizing it, I had pulled up to their driveway. Looking around displayed a scene of peace. Although nothing of importance seemed to be going on, the peaceful tranquility of their neighborhood gave me a sense of overall safety; I truly did miss my childhood home.

Finally hopping out of the car, I proceeded to the front door and immediately pushed my key in.

"There's my pumpkin," greeted my mom the moment I stepped in.

"You must have smelled me coming," I replied, trying to sound as normal as possible.

I didn't want my parents worrying or not being able to sleep because of my carelessness and brought on drama. So, for now at least, I decided to keep my problems to myself.

"I guess I did, something just told me to get up and go check on the pots, that's when I saw you coming up the driveway," she replied before continuing, "It's funny, you were just on my mind. I've just been having an unnerving feeling that I can't seem to shake. I'm just happy that you're okay."

"I'm fine, Mom; you just look for reasons to worry. Everything's okay," I replied as a sinking feeling shot to the bottom of my stomach.

I was always told that mother's knew best. And as my mom appeared to be psychic at times, it was weird that she picked up on the danger that was lurking around me. Her comment only sent my nerves into overdrive. Stepping away to hide any physical reactions, I walked to the back of the house and straight to Mia's room.

Once in Mia's room, we embraced each other as we went on to talk about everything that's been going on with the both of us, everything that is except my near fatal encounter. She filled me in on her plans for the upcoming school year, as she giddily embraced the thought of meeting fresh faces from different parts of the world.

Despite my troubles, seeing the happiness in my sister's face made everything okay again. I was extremely relieved that the relationship with the scumbag had ended, and her focus was back on getting her life started.

The more she talked, the more I saw myself in her. I could just tell that my sister was going to be a split image of me when she got older; it was evident in the way she carried herself and was beginning to think. She wasn't afraid to take chances and speak her mind. She also seemed to have the gifted ability to bounce back from a bad situation a lot quicker than most. While that could be both a blessing and a curse, I could only hope and pray that she would use her strong demeanor and fly girl perception for the greater good.

Continuing to laugh and talk, I was slightly interrupted by the notification of a text. Thinking it may be Karen, I entered my password to check the message and immediately noticed that the text was from an unusual number in a short, irregular sequence. As I read through the text, in a flash my sudden happiness turned into complete fear.

"Are you okay?"asked Mia curiously as she peered at me with a look of concern.

"Yeah, yeah, I just forgot to do something important that I need to take care of," I replied as nonchalantly as possible.

Looking back at the phone in hopes that I had somehow misread it, the inevitable was clear as day. The unknown sender was the Miami-Dade police indicating that the inmate that I was a victim of was recently released.

« CHAPTER 15 »

"LEAH, I SENT YOU AN EMAIL with the conference details and assignments. I just need your departure and arrival dates and preferred travel times," said Jenny as she peeped her head into my office.

"That's right it slipped my mind, I'll try to have that information to you by the end of the day."

"Okay that would be great. I'll start getting the bits and pieces together so I can finalize everything as soon as I get it."

"Awesome. Thanks, Jenny," I replied with a forced smile.

Although extremely helpful, and a damn good secretary, Jenny had a mouth that could run a mile a minute. And I didn't want to give her any indication that I was up for idle conversation. Not to mention she would probably get wind of my unwelcomed drama with Steven, and knowing her, she would probably try to snoop around to find out what's going on. So until things died down, I would make sure that our conversations are chip-chop short.

From the outside I appeared to be coping well with everything, but internally was quite the opposite.

Shortly after getting the text message, I left my parents house and cautiously headed to Karen's. I didn't want any danger that was meant for me to bring harm to my family. Even though I never brought Steven near my parent's house, it would be naïve of me to think that information was private. With just the click of a few buttons he could find out everything he needed to know.

Which is why I feel that Karen's spot is actually perfect. He didn't know much about Karen and only had a first name, so the chance of him finding me there, as far as I am concerned, is presumably slimmer.

But even with Karen's house as a safe haven, the fear was still prominent and lodged in the back of my mind. I had no idea where Steven was, and after blocking all of his numbers, I had no way of knowing what exactly was going through his head. The only way to know for sure about what was really going on would be through Jasmine. Remembering that I told her off and blocked her number, I contemplated on how I would approach her, if at all, with everything that had happened. If Steven was planning something or continuing to talk irrationally, Jasmine would be sure to know. Placing my pride aside, I made it up in my mind to call her as soon as I left work.

Looking at the clock, I realized that it was almost twelve o'clock. Deciding that I would go ahead and take lunch before it got too late, I began the process of logging out of a few open accounts.

As soon as I grabbed my purse from the drawer and retrieved my keys, my phone began to vibrate as it displayed an unusual number. With the area code of 786, I knew that it was a local call, but exactly who was calling brought on feelings of dread. Staring at the phone briefly, I realized that I was getting myself all worked up for what I didn't even know; after all, it could also be a potential client inquiring about business.

"Good afternoon, Leah Miller speaking," I answered trying to hold back any signs of uncertainty.

"Thank God you answered the phone, I've been trying to get a hold of you," replied the caller.

After a brief hesitation, I realized it was Jasmine.

"Jasmine?" I cautiously asked in an attempt for confirmation.

"Yes. Look, I know that things didn't end well with us the last time we met up, but I heard about what happened and I just really felt like I should reach out to you."

Oh, now you do. Fine time, bitch, I thought to myself, doing everything in my power not to blurt it out.

"Jasmine, at this point, I don't know who to trust. I'm still really trying to comprehend and make sense of everything that's going on," I replied.

Placing her on hold, I locked my office and advised the front desk that I would be out for lunch. Once I made it out of the building I resumed the conversation.

"Yeah, I'm back," I managed to say through breaths as I walked towards my car. Carefully looking around, I realized that I made the mistake of not having security escort me to my car. Brushing off my fears, I continued on.

"I just want to say, before I say anything else, that I'm truly sorry for not telling you about the incident that Steven was involved in. I can't help but feel like some of what has happened is my fault."

"So, what exactly have you heard?" I interjected curiously.

After relaying most of the basics, I began tuning her out until she went on to say that she spoke to Steven recently. After that statement was disclosed, I was then all ears.

"I mean, he just continued on and on about how much he cares about you and would never hurt you. He just keeps saying that he wants to talk to you, and what he has to say he's afraid to speak it over the phone, which is why I guess he wants to see you in person. I mean, he was going on and on about secret societies and whatnot, so I kind of started pressuring him to give me a hint of what was so important. But the only thing that I really got out of him, and these were his last words to me before he stormed off, was 'everything and everyone is not always how they seem.'"

Listening on, confirmed by assumptions, it was without question that I was dealing with a nut case. Everything that he apparently said was a blatant cry for attention. Steven simply wanted my attention. The facts said it all and he was right, he was nothing like he seemed.

What was troubling me the most was the fact that he would go to these extremes just to get my attention. I mean, being in love with someone is one thing, but really? Just by me not talking to you the way that I used to brought on an unexpected case of psychosis? Could the actual feelings of love run that deep that all forms of moral reasoning are immediately overshadowed if they become threatened?

Disgusted, yet still fearful, I continued on with the conversation as I made my way out of the parking lot.

"This is really one of those situations that could have been easily avoided if I had known. But this person needs help, Jasmine. As a family friend, you should take the initiative to help him do so, instead of feeding into his idiocy. To be honest with you, I never want to speak to him, let alone see him, ever again. So, from this day forward, it would be in the best interest of all of us if I go my way, and he goes his. And I also want to add that if it's not within the realms of my life being in danger, I never want to speak on this subject again; positive vibes only," I said in an indirect way of cutting them both out of my life.

Once everything was over and done, I plan on giving her my final thoughts on everything that transpired—as well as let her know that my face, name, and everything that she knew about me should be a faded memory. I would never give a snake a second chance to bite me.

After hearing her talk for a few more minutes, I cut her off.

 "Well, Jasmine, I hate that this happened as well, but I'm going to have to talk to you later. I really need to go grab some things before I head back to work."

"Oh, okay, I'm going to let you go, but please give me a call when you get a chance."

"Sure, will do," I replied.

"Wait on it bitch," I murmured as I threw the phone down on the seat.

Within a few short minutes I was pulling up to Igor's. I knew exactly what I needed to help me get through times like this: a few stiff drinks. But seeing that I had to return to work, just two for now would be adequate, I guess; at least to take the edge off.

Igor's was that one spot that was secluded and many people really didn't know about. It was more of an upscale pub that catered to a specific type of crowd. It was also a great meeting spot for single women or those just looking to get lucky. So I knew if I wanted to get away from the typical young Miami crowd, Igor's would be that place.

Sitting in the car, I flipped open my interior mirror just to make sure that I was presentable. With just one quick swipe of my Snob lip gloss by MAC, I was beautified and ready to go. Grabbing the door handle, I stopped dead in my tracks to observe the scene around me before finally stepping out.

Surprisingly, the crowd was larger than I thought it would be. Normally the place was scanty during this time of day and would typically pick up around happy hour. But today there seemed to not be a seat in the house.

Walking to the bar I scanned the area for the perfect spot. Not having many options, I opted for a single stool that sat off to the side of the bar, somewhat in the corner.

As I waited for the bartender's attention, I subconsciously began gazing around the room. The place was packed, but it was mostly old, retired looking men who were all dressed in similar casual clothing: shorts or pants and white polo shirts.

Overly curious, I contemplated on asking the guy beside me what was going on when my thoughts were suddenly interrupted.

"Hey, what can I get for you?" asked the petite, blonde hair bartender.

With her breasts under her chin and her corset cinched at her ribs, it was a wonder how she breathed. I knew that it had to be uncomfortable to walk around all day like a preserved piece of meat sealed in a suction bag.

"Hello. Quick random question, what's going on in here today? It's kind of packed for just lunch." I asked.

"Oh, there's a golf tournament nearby; it's been busy like this since this morning," replied the bartender.

After talking further and ordering my drink, I pulled out my phone and proceeded to check a few emails, when the guy beside me turned around and looked squarely at me, as if he just realized that I was sitting there. Taken aback, I looked at him as I waited for him to speak.

"Well, hello pretty lady, what brings you here today?" asked the strange guy.

"Oh, just stopping by to grab a drink or two, I'm on lunch," I replied as I cursed him internally for asking such an obvious question.

"Nothing wrong with that, is it? I thought you were probably here for the golf tournament. I almost got excited," he continued as he peered at me with his beady, button looking eyes.

Like most of the other patrons, he wore khaki shorts with a white polo that had various symbols embossed in different places. His hair was sandy brown, cut short, and a beige visor hovered over his already creepy eyes.

"Oh no, I'm just slipping in for a drink and then slipping out; no golf for me."

"Well, that's a bummer. Where are my manners? I'm Thomas," replied the apparent golfer as he extended out his hand.

"Nice to meet you, I'm Lilah," I replied, alias in full effect.

"Okay, Lilah. Yeah, everyone knows that if I'm not checking on one of my businesses or working on a deal, I'm somewhere having a drink," he replied through unprecedented laughter.

Still laughing at his own corny joke, he murmured something that I couldn't quite understand. Pretending to be in on the joke, I chuckled slightly hoping that he would soon get it all out and leave me the hell alone.

Saving me from horror, the bartender placed a beautifully decorated martini glass in front of me before smiling and prancing off.

"A martini, huh?" asked the annoying golfer.

"Yeah, one of my faves," I replied with as little enthusiasm as possible.

Immediately getting out of his seat, he placed his drink on the bar top before excusing himself for a bathroom break.

Relieved of his temporary departure, I picked up my drink and began sipping it.

The moment my lip touched the glass, I could smell the fruity alcohol and knew for sure that this drink was exactly what I needed. With just a couple sips, the feeling of relaxation began to come over me. Looking over my glass, I could see the annoying golfer making his way back from the restroom. *What did he do, just go check himself out in the mirror?* I thought to myself.

"Back in record time," he added while pulling out his barstool.

Shooting him a quick smile, I turned my head and pretended to be busy on my phone. I wanted to move, but since there were limited seats and I knew I wouldn't be there much longer, I decided to stay.

After checking emails, texting, and chitchatting briefly with the golfer, I realized that I had been in the bar for almost an hour. Looking up, I signaled the bartender to let her know I was ready to close my tab.

"Leaving so soon? You've only had three drinks."

"Yeah, unfortunately I still have a lot of work to do and that was two too many," I replied.

As the bartender approached my side of the bar to hand me the bill, Thomas reached his hand out as a means of stopping her.

"She won't be needing that, just add her order to my tab," he said to the bartender.

"Not a problem," replied the cheery bartender before prancing away.

"Thank you, you are far too kind," I added with a smile.

"I am, aren't I?" replied Thomas with a failed attempt at being sexy.

As he squinted his eyes and bobbed his head, I took everything in me to maintain my forced smile and calm demeanor. Pulling my chair back, I adjusted my skirt before getting out of my seat.

"Can I walk you to your car?" asked Thomas.

"That's okay, I don't want to bother you, besides you may lose your seat."

"Aw, that's nothing. Look, I just need to have a last glimpse of the prettiest thing that I have seen all year. You really think I rather be in here with a pack of guys?" he chuckled in a low tone of voice.

If pops thinks that we're going to exchange information, he has another thing coming. I could care less how many businesses he runs or what he has; aside from his kind gesture, he definitely made the dry-humor, pest list. Deciding to get it over with once and for all, I agreed to let him walk me out of the pub and to the car.

Leaving the pub with Thomas right behind me, I walked in a fast pace to exemplify my inherent rush.

Continuing to make small talk, I began the process of tuning him out as I consciously checked my surroundings. Finally making to the car, I leaned in forward as I pressed the unlock button on the door handle.

"Well thank...."

I stopped mid sentence as a familiar voice permeated through the air. Looking around anxiously, my heart began to race as I clinched the handle of the door.

Freezing in place, my eyes darted from left to right as I tried to find the location of the dreaded voice. Within a few seconds of looking, Steven darted from behind a black SUV with his face knitted in apparent frustration.

Walking towards me at a fast pace, I regained my composure as I quickly pulled open the door and hopped inside. I immediately locked the doors.

"Wait, hold on, is everything okay?" asked Thomas as Steven approached the front of the car.

"Hey man, this is between me and my lady. You have nothing to do with this bro; just run along and mind your business," yelled Steven.

As he approached the driver's side window of the car, he peered inside before pulling on the handle and then knocking on the glass.

"Open the door!" yelled Steven angrily.

Although obviously angry, he looked confused and disheveled as if he hadn't slept in days.

"This shit is bigger than you could ever imagine. I have some real shit to share with you and all you want to do is run away like a little girl. Here you have a man who really loves you and would put his fucking life on the line for you, and you don't even have the decency to hear what he has to say," he continued.

Turning away from the window, I reminded myself to breathe as the prominent sounds of my heart beating echoed throughout my ears. Pressing firmly on the brakes, I stuck out my shaking sweaty finger as I pressed the button to start the car. With my foot still on the brakes and the gearshift now in reverse, my head quickly swung to the left as the sounds of muffling and commotion drowned out the thuds in my ears.

Looking on in disbelief, I watched as Steven grabbed a hold of Thomas before swiftly shifting his body and forcing Thomas to be in front of him. Wrapping his forearm around his neck, Steven began squeezing tightly in upward motions as he barbarically gritted his teeth in anger.

Almost immediately, the color of Thomas's face went from golden tan to a rosy deep pink. Apparently struggling to breathe, he began rocking his body from left to right in subtle yet intense motions, as he tried desperately to free himself from Steve's apparent ironclad grip.

As he furiously continued squeezing Thomas' neck, my eyes widened as my mouth slowly fell open. Where was everyone? Didn't anybody see the ruckus that was going on?

With my mind going a hundred miles an hour, sweat began to pop out of my pores as I contemplated on what to do next. Continuing to look around I could see no one in sight. Not a single person appeared to be in the distance. With Steven's forearm clinched around Thomas's neck, the gradual limp and slow movements of his arms and legs signified that he only had a little fight left in him.

As if something came over me, my feelings of fear quickly began turning into anger and disgust. How long could I sanely continue living like this? At what point would it all end?

Subconsciously liberated, I grabbed a hold of the gearshift as I angrily threw it back into park. Reaching for the door handle, I instantly remembered that Karen had slipped a can of mace into my purse just days before. Letting go of the handle, I reached over for my purse as I feverishly began searching for the little black can. As if luck was on my side, almost immediately I could feel what I knew had to be it. Pulling it out, I positioned my fingers on the pump as I readily reached back across the car for the door handle.

Like a trained militant, I quickly scrunched downwards as I slipped my body through the crack that I made in the door. Within seconds I was eye to eye with the man that seemed hell bent on ruining my life. The mere sight of his eyes intensified my anger. Without hesitation and without giving it any further thought, I swiftly pulled back my arm and immediately lunged forward, hitting Steven dead square in the face.

Acknowledging the fact that I was at a point of no return, I began thrusting my hand against his head in forceful, pounding motions. With each powerful thrust, I could hear the hardened aluminum as it vigorously pinged off the sides of his head.

In a lightening quick move, Steven quickly released Thomas from his grasp and began holding the sides of his own head in apparent pain. With Thomas now free and Steven slightly injured, I stopped briefly to catch my breath as I mentally prepared for what was to come. Through aspirated breaths, I kept my eyes fixated on Steven while slowly backing away from the scene.

Still clutching the side of his head, he began staggering around as if the hits made him dazed. Fearing his next move, I methodically veered behind a car that was near as I crept slowly back towards the entrance of the pub.

"Call 911! Someone just got attacked outside and he might be on his way in here," I yelled the moment I entered inside.

While running towards the back of the bar, I looked around feverishly for an exit door. Conveniently placed across from the bathrooms, I stood near the back entrance so that I could get a clear, yet discreet view of the entrance.

By this point the pub was in chaos. More than half of the chairs were empty as golfers filled the sidewalk and front entrance. With the sound of loud chatter and screeching chairs muffling the outdoor voices, it became difficult for me to know exactly what was going on.

The feeling of uncertainty left me panting. Did someone get a hold of Steven or did he get away? Would he come rushing inside looking for me? As panicking thoughts entered my mind, I began tapping my body to see if I had my cell phone.

"Damn it," I whispered. I had left my entire purse and cell phone in the car. If Steven got a hold of it, or worse yet my car keys, I would be doomed. He would have access to my house, office, and a number of other things. Tapping my foot in panic, I picked my brain on what I should do next.

Suddenly, a loud crashing sound rang through the building. Carefully peeping around the corner, I quickly realized that the place had practically gone empty. Noticing movement near the bar, I could see the bartender crouched in the corner as she held her cell phone tightly to her ear.

With the feelings of liberation slowly slipping away, I began praying, pleading that I got out of this horrific situation without being harmed. I didn't know where Steven was, what else he had done, and what else he had in store for me.

« CHAPTER 16 »

"HOW MUCH LONGER IS IT going to be? All of my tests came back normal and I'm still here an hour later," I said to the ER nurse through the bedside intercom.

"The nurse should be in any minute now with your discharge information and instructions," she replied.

"Well, I'll be right here waiting," I replied sarcastically.

I hated hospitals and the annoying sound of monitors and doctors buzzing about the place. The room was ice cold, my phone had no internet connection, and I was hungry for real food.

"Thanks a lot, Steven; job well done," I mumbled to myself.

Thankfully, Steven was back in jail and probably wouldn't be getting out anytime soon for violating his no contact order.

As a laid in the bed, the bits and pieces that I could remember began to play back in my mind. It seemed like within just a few minutes of feeling faint as I stood at the back exit, I heard the distinct sounds of police cars and ambulances swirling in the distance. Relieved, I waited anxiously until I knew for sure that the scene was safe.

Running outside to meet with the cops and observe the scene, I saw Steven with his face pushed into the ground and three older men hovering over him. Thomas was sitting upright in an adjacent car with several other patrons talking to him and giving him water.

The entire scene was total chaos. There were cop cars everywhere, a fire truck, ambulance and groups of sightseers huddled from the sidewalk all the way to the road. As I tried to relay to the police the details of what had transpired, it became increasingly difficult to speak and subsequently breathe. Although the scene was controlled and Steven was in cuffs, I still found it difficult to calm myself as my heart continued pounding rapidly.

Realizing my apparent franticness, the police called over the radio for an additional ambulance. As I sat in my car awaiting medical attention, I could see the first set of EMTs as they rendered services to Thomas before sliding him inside the ambulance. Noticing that he was responding to their commands and questions, I knew that things weren't as bad as they previously had appeared.

The next thing I knew, I woke up in a hospital bed with breathing tubes, monitors, and two female officers standing over me. I went on to explain to them what happened and wrote a statement detailing what I could remember.

"Leah?" said the nurse as he pulled back the curtain and peeped his head in.

"Yup, that's me," I replied.

"Alrighty, the doctor went over all the tests and everything did come back normal. It appears that what you experienced was a stress induced anxiety attack. The doctor wants you to follow up with you personal care physician in no more than three days. Any questions?"

"Nope, not at all. I'm just really ready to get out of here," I replied.

"I understand, but unfortunately someone is going to have to pick you up. You were given sedatives that cause drowsiness, so we cannot let you leave the hospital alone."

After debating with the nurse a little longer, I decided that there was no winning. With the decision to still not get my parents involved, I gave the nurse Karen's number so that she could arrange for her to pick me up. After unhooking all of my monitors, the nurse left the room as I began flipping through the TV channels.

Hearing voices in the room, I looked up and realized that it was Karen and two other nurses. Impressed at her quick arrival, I looked down at my watch and I realized that it was almost nine o'clock; I had slept for over two hours!

"Thank God you're here," I said to Karen as I began trying to get off of the bed.

"Oh my God, Leah, I'm just happy that you're okay. This is crazy," she replied.

Once we got everything in order, I was wheeled out of the hospital and straight to Karen's awaiting car.

During the drive to Karen's house, we discussed everything that went on that day and how Steven had just appeared out of nowhere. Visually upset, Karen relayed her feelings and offered several alternatives to help cope with the problem. It was just like Karen to take a manly approach to situations and take matters into her own hands. I just wanted the situation to diffuse without adding more fuel to the fire by causing harm to anyone else.

Once at Karen's, I showered, ate, and popped open a bottle of wine to relax. Sitting on the couch and glancing through my phone, I realized that I had two different messages from Chanlor that I had received earlier that evening. In one of the messages he said that he was planning on leaving tomorrow to go back to the UK; as well as how much he couldn't wait to finally see me.

Excited about the one thing that seemed to be going right, I decided to return his calls immediately before it got even later.

Answering only after the second ring, was the undeniably voice of pure British sexiness.

"Hey, baby!" I yelled out excitedly.

"Darling, why are you're so difficult to reach these days?" asked Chanlor.

Before being able to respond, I could see Karen in the background making silly faces and snickering. Fanning her off, I put my hand over the receiver as I playfully mouthed the words 'screw you' before walking out the room.

"Oh my God, today was crazy, baby. We had meetings back to back and once that was over, I had to run over to my friend's house for support. This guy that she was dating just started acting erratic out of the blue; it was really crazy," I replied in a theatrical manner that would probably impress the most seasoned actress.

"Oh boy, that really does sound like quite a day. Is everything okay with your friend now?" he asked, sounding really concerned.

"Yes, yes. The police were called and he was whisked away, so everything is good for now."

"Very good," he replied.

"Buuut, on another and more positive note, I absolutely can't wait to finally see you. It's been way too long, babe," I added in soft and sexy monotone.

"You can't imagine how much it's killing me not to have you here. If it wasn't for this last minute business trip, you would be in my arms right now, with a bottle of Bollinger sitting next to us and a nice flick playing on the telly."

"Hmm, exactly my kind of night," I said, bubbly.

"Very, very soon. As I said, I will be flying out first thing in the morning, so I should be home by mid-evening. You are welcome to make plans from tomorrow onward," added Chanlor.

"Okay that's actually perfect. I have a business conference to attend in New York a week from today, so I'll probably just fly from there and come straight to you."

"Very well. Just give me the flight details and I'll have one of my drivers grab you up from the airport."

The sound of his accent and boss like demeanor made me quiver with each pitch of his voice.

After talking a little further, we were forced to end the conversation due to an incoming call from one of his men that was left to handle his businesses. Understanding its importance, I reassured him that I would give him a call tomorrow as soon as I thought he was home.

Once I hung up the phone, I sat in the dark quiet room as I tried to make sense of everything that had happened. Being involved with Chanlor, even just speaking to him, gave me a sense of overall relief. It was like a breath of fresh air. But I couldn't help but wonder why someone as negative as Steven came into my life. Was this whole escapade punishment for something wrong I had done in the past? And why didn't I pick up on any of the usual signs that crazies are known to show?

Continuing to sit there, I replayed various scenes in my mind to see where things went wrong. I analyzed every comment, action, and gesture that came to mind, only to still be left in a haze.

Realizing that I was prolonging the terror, I made up my mind once and for all to not let Steven's motives and actions get the best of me. If I had to purchase a firearm or just move altogether, I was willing to do whatever it took to regain my sense of peace.

I had too much to look forward to and too many ways to add to my happiness. Hell, if I played my cards right, I might not even come back to the United States. Hopefully by the time Steven sees me again, I'll be English royalty and a force to not be reckoned with.

∞∞∞

For the next week, things seem to go perfectly back normal. Steven was held without bond and luckily won't be a threat anytime soon. Following the incident, I updated Merlich on what transpired and told him that I would be taking a couple personal days off to clear my mind.

During my extra time off I scheduled a hair appointment, spa day, and even managed to visit my aunt and uncle at their newly built home. Since the New York trip was quickly approaching, Karen decided to take a couple days off with me for emotional support and shopping. But instead of staying in for a day or two and relaxing like I intended, we have been from Ft. Lauderdale to West Palm Beach and back, running errands and handling business

Now anyone that knows Karen knows that she is always about her business. She was always looking for a new way to make another dollar. She may not be Fortune 500 material, but she sure as hell had motives that could land her a seat at the table. For that very reason I respected and loved her.

Despite all the recent drama with Steven, I was finally beginning to feel like the old Leah again. I guess the incident was just one of those wrenches that life could sometimes throw your way. But I was always told, since childhood, that I was a very strong and determined person. And that very strength and determination is undoubtedly what made me the woman that I have become.

As I sat in passenger side of Karen's car while at a red light, I gazed out the window as I admired two moms with strollers as they happily pushed them along. The visual made me think about my future and if I would ever have kids. It was no secret that I wasn't getting any younger, and I definitely didn't want to be a grandma just trying to have children. I was finished with school, deep into my career, and getting emotionally tired of playing the field.

In just my short time of getting back on the scene, I have met a manic, a broke loser and have been hit with various other offers that just never made the team. I couldn't help but wonder if these were all signs for me to slow things down and focus on what was really real. The emotional rollercoaster of carrying on multiple engagements was just becoming too much for me to handle. In more ways than one, it was actually counterproductive to my overall goal.

"What are you over there thinking about?" asked Karen, interrupting my thoughts.

"What makes you say that?"

"I know you, Leah. I know that once you get quiet and start staring off, you have something deep on your mind. So let it out, what's going on?"

Chucking slightly, I replied. "I was just thinking about everything that's been happening from Steven to the incident with Mia. It's like the pool of men that we have to pick from is full of, well, nothing."

"Girl, tell me something new! That's why we are the way we are. Hellooo, where is Leah is and what happened to her?" she added jokingly.

"No, I mean in that sense I know, but it's just like geesh, it really is crazy out here. I'm tired, right now I'm really hoping that everything works out with Chanlor and it's happily ever after. If not, I don't think I can go through another 'getting to know you stage,' I might just give up and get a few cats and grow old with them and say 'Fuck it!'"

Turning to look at each other, we both burst out in laughter.

"All I can say is that I've tried and tried again, even recently, with that bum ass wannabe mechanic. And each and every time I was met with almost the same bullshit. So as of now, I throw my hands up. I understand that you're really feeling this guy Chanlor, and if he's what you want and you trust your judgment, then go for it. He might just be the outlet you've been looking for," replied Karen before continuing, "But I'm letting you know right now that if you move to the UK, damn it, I'm coming with you!"

As we continued driving along, we laughed and gossiped just like the old times. It was always refreshing to get her view on certain matters. Because as she always says, if you don't want the honest truth, then don't ask. And I knew that with Karen, I would be getting my tea served as is.

After driving for a while, I realized that we had made it to a strange looking house closer south.

"What's here?" I asked curiously.

"Just got to meet with my Spanish papi about some potential business," replied Karen.

"Karen, I hope you're not...."

"Don't worry, it's nothing like that, I just came to talk to him in person," she replied, opening the car door.

Looking around, I began to check out the scene. The house had an eerily, weird look to it and the multitude of moss-covered trees that hung over it certainly didn't help. Quite frankly, the house was an absolute mess. In the distance I could see several little kids standing in the middle of the street while cars sped up and down the road with no care in the world. As I sat there, I began to feel uneasy. This was definitely not a neighborhood that I would frequent. It just seemed like everyone that passed by was up to no good or had ill intentions.

Seeing the door crack open, I was relieved to know that we would finally be leaving. But instead of it being Karen, out came a dark haired slender guy who had the looks of a mafia hit man. Once he shut the door, his eyes stood focus on the car as he walked closer and closer. Finally approaching the car, he stood by the window as he looked inside with an emotionless, daring stare.

What the hell has Karen gotten me into? I thought nervously to myself. Unsure of what to do, I decided to roll down the window to see what his business was.

"Who are you?" asked the guy the moment I rolled down the window.

Under normal circumstances, I would have corrected him and asked him who the hell was he, but my mom certainly didn't raise a fool. I was not about to say anything that could potentially tick him off.

"Hey, I'm Chanay," I replied as cheerfully as I could, praying that he didn't have prior knowledge on my real name.

"Who else is in the car? Roll down all the windows and open the trunk," he added, still showing no emotions and barely moving his lips.

I began unbuckling my seat belt to do as I was asked.

"Hold your hands up and don't make any fast movements!" yelled out the guy.

"I have nothing but cards on me. If you want, you can have everything in my purse," I added, nervously trying not to panic.

"Hold your hands up while you reach over, just make sure I can see them."

Throwing up my arms, I made it obvious that I had nothing in my hands and no intentions on trying anything. When I noticed the front door of the house slowly creep open. As I unlocked all the doors, I could see Karen from the side of my eye slowly emerging from the house. Deep-seated panic quickly turned into relief as I realized that she was alone and free to help. Placing my hands back in a surrendering motion, I slowly reverted my body back into its previous position, being careful not to make any sudden movements.

"What the hell is going on?" asked Karen as she approached the car. "Seaman, I hope you're not out here harassing my friend now," she continued.

As if it were a light switch, the strange looking guy who appeared so mean and heartless, burst out laughing uncontrollably.

"Damn, why did you have to come out here and fuck everything up? I had her," said the guy through his laughter.

If looks could kill, he would surely be dead. There are a million and one ways to garner someone's attention and unnecessarily freighting them sure as hell is not one of them. Now pissed more than ever, I glanced at him briefly before quickly turning my head away. I was all for jokes, but unbeknownst to him, this was definitely not the time for scare tactics.

"Ha, ha, ha," I finally blurted out.

"I am so done with you, man. Don't worry, he did me the very same way the first time I came here," added Karen as she giggled slightly.

"I'm sorry, mama, I just like to have a little fun every now and then; I didn't scare you too much, did I?" he said.

"I can't with you right now. You're going to have me on blood pressure pills with your games," I replied with a slight smirk, still upset yet relieved at the same time.

 "Look, we've got to run, I'll see you later. You play absolutely too much. And you better stop that shit before you scare the wrong person; everyone's strapped these days," added Karen as she backed out of the driveway.

"You know I'm about whatever," he jokingly replied.

As we backed out of the driveway, I gave Karen the 'what the hell just happened' look.

"Don't feel bad, he got me the very same way and I was scared shitless. To be honest, I can't believe they have him playing around like that because the dude that owns that house is about his business—when he's coming for you, he's not coming on the playing tip at all," she replied.

As Karen's phone suddenly began ringing, I could see a smile spread widely across her face as she pressed the talk button.

"Hey babe," she answered.

"Nothing much, just out with Leah having a little lunch," she added while looking over at me smiling.

After being on the phone for a few short minutes, the call came to an end.

"So, that was your boy," added Karen before continuing, "I think he's getting ready to call you; he was saying something about the trip and some lady name Jenny."

As soon as she finished her last words, my phone began to ring. Looking down, I realized that it was in fact Merlich.

"Yup, this is him now. 'Hello, Leah speaking,'" I answered.

"Hey Leah, did Jenny contact you by any chance?" asked Merlich.

"No, I haven't heard from her; what's going on?"

"Well, I thought she would have contacted you by now. I guess she got busy with you being out and everything being busy around here. Anyway, the hotel where the conference is being held is booked completely. It looks like people booked their rooms way ahead of time, because I ended up having to get a two bedroom suite due to all the single rooms being unavailable."

"You cannot be serious."

"Yeah, unfortunately. And all of the other nearby hotels is booked out as well. The ones that do have availability are a little too far out, in my opinion. But this doesn't necessarily have to be a problem. If you don't have a problem staying with Karen and I, I certainly don't mind and I'm sure she definitely doesn't mind. I mean, we do have an extra bedroom and it's basically just going to be there unoccupied. And what's good about it is if everything happens that way, you can save your lodging funds and use them for something else."

"Umm, geesh, this is so unexpected and last minute," I finally managed to say.

As I sat there with the phone to my ear, I felt cornered and caught off guard. It was important that I attend the conference as the extra networking would be great for my career, but I would literally be lodging with my boss. Not to mention he and Karen's previous advances.

"Hmmm. Well, it doesn't seem like I have much of a choice right now," I added with a suppressed laugh before continuing, "But I don't see it being a problem—why not I mean, we're all adults, I'm sure we can share a space for a week and not kill each other; I think it will be fun, actually."

After going over a few extra details regarding the conference, we ended the call.

The moment my finger hit the end button, I started contemplating on how the trip would turn out and if I had made the right decision.

This should be fun and interesting, I thought to myself. *Very interesting.*

« CHAPTER 17 »

RIIING RANG THE ALARM, signaling me to get out of bed.

Reaching over, I silenced it as I moaned and groaned at the horrendous God-awful sound. In my world, there was never a good reason to have to get up before 7 a.m.; it just wasn't in my DNA.

Despite my apparent upset, it was a must that I get up and get things going. Our flight was scheduled to leave at 10:45, and with the snotty TSA agents it was crucial that we leave the house at a reasonable time.

Peeling myself out of bed, I peeped down the hallway to see if Karen was up and around.

"Karen! Wake up! We have less than an hour to get dressed and get out of here," I yelled aloud, knowing my voice would amplify through the tiny apartment.

"Shut up!" replied Karen as she tried yelling in a muffled voice.

Within forty-five minutes we were both dressed and ready to head out. Deciding that Uber would be faster than a cab, I tracked down an available car a made arrangements for pick up.

I hate airports; they are always a cluster fuck of cab cars, buses, and a multitude of other vehicles riding bumper to bumper. But with the type of lifestyle that I lived, I had no choice but to frequent them. So until I was able to book private flights with concierge service, buzzing through an airport was just something I would have to get used to; and the way things were going for me, I know that will only be temporary.

∞∞∞

By 6:12 p.m. and Karen and I were finally checked in and relaxing. Merlich was due to fly in later on tonight, so at least we would be able to have the place to ourselves until then.

"Let's go down to little Italy, there's a really cool Oriental-American spot there that I like," I said to Karen as we lay poolside at the hotel, sipping frozen piña coladas.

"I don't know if I'm feeling Oriental food right now, maybe something else," she replied.

"Aw, c'mon, it's just one meal out of many. Besides, they cook mostly American food with a twist of Chinese; trust me, you'll like it."

"Ugh, really, Leah?" added Karen before continuing, "I guess I can try it, but tomorrow I pick the spot; no complaints."

As we lay out on the elongated pool chairs, I continued sipping my frozen drink as I admired the peaceful scenery.

The Olympic size swimming pool glistened with vivid shades of blue as the sun's bright rays bounced off of it. The hotel's antique décor and prestigious ambience only amplified and perfected the scene, giving off a fulfilled feeling of royalty. Being that it was a weekday, there weren't many people around, and the ones that were there seemed to be in out business. Apart from two or three other families that appeared to be on vacation, Karen and I pretty much had the full attention of all the outdoor staff.

After laying there, chitchatting and drinking until dusk, we decided to get up and head out on the town for a real bite to eat. The food at the poolside bar was just not going to get it; that good New York cuisine was definitely calling our names.

Fortunately for us, I made reservations with a car company so that we would have the luxury of curbside service as we made our way around the city. The moment we stepped out the front door of the hotel, a car was there patiently waiting.

"Ms. Miller?" asked the driver.

"Yes, it is," I quickly inserted.

"Right this way," he replied as he ushered me and Karen into the back seat of the black town car.

"I can get used to this," added Karen as she made herself comfortable in the seat.

Cruising through the east side of Manhattan, I breathed a sigh of relief as I admired the lights, entertainment, and New York nightlife. Most of the funny characters working for tips were gone, and patrons that were apparently seeking the nightlife engulfed the streets, both in cars and on foot. Finally making it to our spot, we pulled up beside a row of cars that were parked alongside the street side. Blocking them in, the driver quickly hopped out and ushered us inside the restaurant.

"Welcome to the Bacchanal New York, do you have reservations?" asked the well-dressed host.

"Yes, we do, the Miller party of two," I replied.

After reviewing a long list of names, he directed us to a small, cozy table near the rear of the restaurant.

"Your waiter will be with you shortly."

"I must admit when you said Oriental-American I was thinking one of those spots that served that same fried rice crap, but this place is actually nice," said Karen as we made our selves comfortable at the table.

"It is; you should know by now that my restaurant picks are always the best. But the first time that I tried it was in Vegas; I've been in love ever since."

Once the waiter took our drink orders, we made our way to the multitude of buffet tables as we prepared salads and appetizers for the table.

"I'm surprised that I haven't heard from Robert yet, he should be here by now. If he doesn't call soon, I'm going to have to call and check up on him, or at least make sure that his flight made it," added Karen as she flared her napkin before placing it on her lap.

"I was getting ready to ask you who the hell was Robert, until it hit me that Merlich's first name was actually Robert," I replied before continuing, "You guys are getting really close now, I see."

"Well, like I said, he seems to actually be a really nice guy, but you already know my sole motive. Don't get it twisted, nothing has changed," added Karen as she peered at me with the *eye*.

"I just have to do what I have to do to accomplish the things I need to accomplish. Anything extra is welcomed, but not necessary," she continued.

"I hear ya."

"Hey, what do you think about that guy over there?" asked Karen in between bites.

"What guy?" I asked curiously, looking slightly to my side.

"The guy over there sitting by himself; he looks wealthy and lonely," added Karen as she nudged her head towards the right side of the room.

Veering my head slightly, I gazed nonchalantly in the direction of the guy in question. Sitting at a table directly across from us was an older looking man dressed in a nice gray suit, which without a doubt appeared expensive. Directly in front of him was a tablet and two cell phones that he couldn't seem to put down, even while he was eating.

"Okay, what about him? There are hundreds of business men lurking around New York, what's so special about him?" I asked.

"Yeah, but the object of the game is to seize every opportunity. This is a perfect chance for you to go introduce yourself and try to, as you would say, network."

"Karen, really? You expect me to just walk up and introduce myself out of the blue?"

"That's exactly the problem with some of us women. We're so hung up on what society expects and what's more traditional that we missed these very opportunities. What's so wrong with you approaching a man that appears to have potential?" added Karen.

After clearing my throat and taking a sip of wine, I continued. "I never said that anything was wrong with it, I just personally prefer to be the hunted rather than the hunter. I feel that I just have an advantage in the situation. Besides, after everything that just happened, I'm taking a break on meeting anyone new; at least for the moment. I honestly feel that I should just use my energy for my career and my extra attention for Chanlor," I continued.

"I hear ya, but let me ask you a question: Are you into Chanlor because of the money or do you really like him for who he is?"

"Both. I mean he's a really cool guy; he makes me laugh, he's attentive, and always makes sure that I'm good on every end."

"Well, you never know, he may just be the one, but keep your eyes open and your ears in tune. Just keep in mind our motto: *When the money games and the bullshit begins, we're out before your pockets can shout,*" added Karen, tilting her head to the side as a gesture of conformation.

Covering my mouth with the napkin, I burst out in laughter. It was amazing that she still remembered our so-called motto, since we had made it just weeks after starting our first year of high school together. Even then, we were young hustlers on a mission, destined to grab our piece of the American pie. And although many years have passed, the motive undeniably remains the same.

Continuing to eat and chat, we began reminiscing about the good old days and how we used to run games on unsuspecting victims. Remembering the way things were definitely makes me appreciate our growth and maturity. Even though the path may seem dim at times and may seem like we're covering no territory, a quick reflection of the past can be the best measurement of personal progress. Looking back at my life thus far, I am pleased with the woman I have become and to be honest, I wouldn't change a minute of it for the world.

Finishing up dinner, we made contact with our driver to let him know that we were almost done. Within ten minutes or so, I received a text from the driver indicating that he was outside.

"Okay, he's here, let's go," I said to Karen as I rose from my seat, placing the napkin on the table.

"So, where to?" she asked. "We can't just go back to the hotel like that. Besides, Robert just texted and said that he just made it to the room. So, he needs some time to relax before having our loud asses in there."

"Well, there is this really cool spot that we can hit up that's not too far from here."

"Let's do it!" added Karen excitedly.

Walking towards the front, we waved good-bye to the handsome host as we made our way to the awaiting car.

"Madams," said the driver as he ushered us inside of the town car.

"The lower east side, please; Bowery Ballroom," I relayed to the driver.

"Certainly. Quite a few people are going there tonight as well, I've heard. I think there is a popular band expected to be there tonight," replied the driver.

"Well, there you go, I guess we came at the right time," I happily added.

As we pulled up to our destination, a long line of patrons lined the side of the building to the corner.

"Look at that damn line!" said Karen with a slight escalation in her voice.

"Relax. I have everything covered. I have a friend that promotes in this area and I made sure to tell him that I would be up for the week, so I'm sure that he can get us in before the crowd; as well as a table and bottle service," I added as I picked up my cell phone.

Dialing up my New York connection, I informed him that we were outside of Bowery and needed help getting past the large crowd.

Lucky for us, he was at the Bowery for the night and could meet us at the entrance in a few minutes. Shortly after, I got a text from him instructing us to make our way to the door on the left side of the building, near the front entrance.

"Leah, you get better and better every time that I see you," said my old friend Roderick as he greeted Karen and I at the entrance.

"Rod, how are you babe? It's been so long," I replied as we tightly embraced each other with a hug.

After releasing me, he stood in place as he starred into my eyes.

"Oh, Rod, this is my best friend Karen, and Karen, this is my very good friend Roderick," I quickly added in an attempt to break the awkward stare.

"Nice to meet you," said Rod as he stuck out his hand for a handshake.

"Nice to meet you as well," Karen replied with a smile as they shook hands.

"Alright, so I got you two ladies nice upper tier seating with nearby curtains for privacy, as well as private bottle and drink service."

"You're the man Rod," I quickly inserted with a smile.

Following his lead, we veered towards a flight of stairs that sat near the rear of the building. Once upstairs, we were greeted with an array of luxury, as several velvet couches outlined the upper tier, with matching velvet curtains hanging in the distance.

"Okay, here we are. I think Julie is the bartender tonight for this section, so I'll go let her know to take good care of you."

After verifying that we were okay, Roderick took off to a section near the front of the bar. The bar's blue neon backlighting stood out like a line of laser beams as it bounced off the disco lighting flashing from below. The upstairs dimly lit interior created a scene that was cozy, yet vividly lively and entertaining. Immediately taking a seat, I breathed out a sigh of relief as my body sank into the plush material of the couch.

"Let's just order a bottle of Henny, and maybe a bottle of champagne later," I yelled to Karen as I leaned closer to her ear.

From the moment we started drinking, I knew that it was going to be one of those wild and crazy nights. From drinking all day by the pool, to sipping wine at the Bacchanal, and now in the process of downing an entire bottle of Hennessy, things were sure to be interesting.

As we partied to the sounds of a well-known band, we drank and laughed as the vibes became more and more intense. By this point I knew I had definitely had more than enough to drink, but the feeling of being away from home removed all sense of responsibility; I felt as free as if I didn't have a care in the world. Picking up the bottle from the ice tub, I threw back my head as I put the bottle to my mouth and guzzled down what was probably the equivalent of at least two shots of liquor. Turning to Karen, I motioned my hands in a sporadic pointing motion, promoting her to do the same.

As neighboring sections looked on, Karen bent her head backwards as I poured the liquor directly down her throat. Now seemingly the center of attention, we swirled and danced as the vibrations of the music intensified the euphoric feeling.

Standing near the rails and looking down at the hyped crowd below, things began to appear hazy as my body felt jittery, like I needed to keep moving. Turning around to Karen, I smiled widely as she began making her way back towards the rails with a freshly made drink in her hand.

"I think we need to leave, I feel like I can't stop moving, but my feet are killing me. And before you say it, I am not under any circumstances taking off my shoes," I said to Karen as I held the rail tightly with my left hand.

Appearing to be in a drunken haze, Karen leaned forward and smiled as she took a sip of her drink. Noticing that my voice had a slur and Karen was at the brink of destruction, I knew that it was time to call a halt to the party.

"I'm calling the driver; I don't think I can take anymore!" I yelled as I pushed my mouth closer to Karen's ears.

Fumbling around my purse for my phone, I texted the driver to let him know that we were ready to be picked up. Grabbing Karen by the arm, we walked side-by-side, using our bodies to hold each other up as we made our way towards the stairs.

"You ladies need a ride?" asked a strange looking guy as he leaned towards my ear.

"Not at all!" I yelled aloud.

Continuing to hold on to each other, we made our way down the stairs and out of the building. As soon as we stepped outside, the first thing that caught my eye was the black town car and our driver sitting in the driver's seat. Apparently, just realizing who we were, he immediately hopped out of the car as he made his way towards the sidewalk to assist us.

"Here, just hold on to my right hand, and, madam, hold on to the left. The car is right this way," said the driver as he ushered us to the car like teenagers rolling in from a wild night out.

Slumping into the leather seats of the car, I quickly unbuckled the sides of my heels as the numbness in my foot became almost unbearable.

"Damn, I wasn't ready to leave yet! What happened?" yelled Karen as if I was a mile away.

"You're drunk and it's late. Let's just go back to the hotel," I inserted assertively.

Grunting, but apparently deciding not to speak further, she removed her shoes as she slanted her body towards the middle console. After a few minutes, I breathed a long sigh of relief as I saw the bright lighting of the hotel lights.

Getting out at the entrance, I assured the driver that I would be using him for the remainder of the week and would handle the billing details with the company in the morning.

 "Alright, time for bed," I added as I slid the card in and out of the hotel door. Flashing green, I pulled on the door handle and made my way inside.

"Well, hello ladies, again we meet," said Merlich smiling as he sat on the sofa shirtless, with a drink in his hand.

"Hey, baby!" shouted Karen, running and jumping into his arms.

Quickly looking away, I murmured under my breath at the sight of his small necklace nestled on top of his thick, coiled looking chest hairs.

"Oh, hey Robert," I added.

"You ladies look like you had a great time," said Merlich with a comical smile.

"A really great time," I replied dramatically. " But I think my body needs rest now."

Reverting to the chaise that sat adjacent to the sofa, I kicked off my heels as I slowly ran my fingers up and down my feet, creating a relaxing and calming effect. Although my feet couldn't take the stress of another pair of heels, my body was still infused with alcohol and the sounds of the band continued to play in my head.

"Aw, don't be ridiculous, the night is still young, and just think about it, we technically don't have work for a week. So why not enjoy the time," Merlich quickly added.

Rising from the seat, he walked over to the kitchen and pulled out a bottle of Kros champagne from the hotel's silver wine cooler.

"Ladies?" said Merlich as he held the green chilled bottle of champagne in the air.

"Oh, yes, a perfect night-cap. Any champagne glasses, or just wine glasses?" asked Karen as she sprang up from the sofa and headed to the kitchen.

Knowing that we had consumed a variety of different alcohols, my mind wanted desperately for everything to end. But my body and my inner party girl really didn't want the excitement to stop.

"Count me in," I blurted out as I glanced briefly in the direction of the kitchen.

Rumbling through my clutch, I retrieved my cell phone and began going through text messages and emails.

 "Okay, a cold glass of champagne for you," said Karen in a low, yet unusual tone of voice.

Snapping out of my haze, I reached out my hand for the glass before slowly lifting my head. The moment my eyes made contact with Karen's, I was immediately taken back by what was in front of me.

Diverting my eyes from her fixated stare, I gradually lowered them as the details and motives of her attire became all the more apparent. Outfitted in an all black lace top and bottom, adorned together with thigh high stockings and garter belt, stood my best friend of more than fifteen years.

« Chapter 18 »

"Well, you did say that you were up for a little champagne, right?" asked Karen as she stood in front of me.

"Umm, sure. I just didn't imagine that it would be delivered in a negligee," I replied sarcastically as I adjusted myself in the lounge.

"Oh, my outfit? I just wanted to be a little more comfortable, that's all," she replied nonchalantly.

As I took the glass from Karen, a million thoughts began to flood my mind. Looking for answers, I looked over at Merlich who I realized was rumbling in the refrigerator as if nothing out of the ordinary was happening.

Sipping on her own glass of champagne, Karen reverted to the couch near the TV that she and Merlich originally shared. The look on her face and her overall calm demeanor displayed a different side of her that I obviously never knew existed. Just a few years ago, she scorned me when she found out that I was attending swinger's parties with Charles. And now she was acting as if it was commonplace to fro lock in front of your man and best friend, half dressed in skimpy lingerie.

Finally leaving the kitchen, Merlich plopped down in the couch next to Karen as he gazed unflappably at the television. With only the sound of the TV beaming through the room, the atmosphere became awkward and chilling as the feelings of uncertainty began to set in.

"Hey Leah, let's step out on the balcony for a little fresh air and girl talk," said Karen.

Great idea, I thought to myself as I rose from the chair.

Once on the balcony, the fresh, chilled air crept quietly under my leather-frilled skirt. Breathing inwardly, I took deep shallow breaths as I took in the calming scene.

"What a freaking night," I said as we pulled up the balcony chairs to take a seat.

"Tell me about it."

Simultaneously sipping our champagne, we sat briefly before Karen started repositioning to face me.

"I really have something to come clean about," said Karen as she starred into my eyes.

Unsure how to respond, I observed her facial features briefly as I searched for any clues as to what could be next. Staring keenly, she squinted her eyes as an unusual, quirky smile slowly spread across her face.

"Oh God, I'm not even sure if I'm ready to hear it, but go ahead let me have it," I said.

"Umm well, I really don't know any other way to say this but, I...I...I've secretly had a crush on you since our college days," added Karen nervously.

"A crush? What do you mean a crush? Maybe it's just the alcohol, Karen," I replied, confused and not sure what to make of her confession.

"No. These are feelings that I've had for quite some time now, Leah. I've always secretly looked up to you and admired how you seem to be so accomplished and always put together. It's like you set out to do something and no matter what, it just always works out for you. I mean, you have your career, you own your home, a great family, and not to mention men who seem to adore you; it's just sexy to me," said Karen before continuing, "To be honest, I don't know how I feel right now. I love you as a friend, but those feelings, along with my lifelong curiosity about women, kind of made me secretly fall in love you over the years. I just could never bring myself to tell you."

As I continued listening, I was speechless. I've known Karen almost all of my life, and I've never heard her speak about her feelings the way she is now. She always seemed so hardcore and straight to the point; it was if she felt nothing.

"Wow, Karen, I'm really at a loss for words right now. I...I mean, I just don't know what to say, really," I replied as I began looking around.

After a few moments had passed, Karen slowly rose from her seat and began passionately kissing me on the lips. Frozen in my chair and taken back by her sudden boldness, I continued sitting there without as much as moving my lips.

Reaching out her hand, she fondly began caressing my breasts, rubbing them slowly and methodically as she squeezed and pulled at my nipples. Cradling my jaw with one hand, she continued her fondling actions; the sensations caused my breathing to get deeper and deeper.

The softness of her hand and the invigorating feeling of her touch made me question everything I knew to be true. I've never had fantasies of being with another woman, nor has it ever crossed my mind. Especially with my best friend.

Running her fingers down my skirt, she firmly grabbed my thighs, squeezing them as she methodically made her way to my inner thighs. Anticipating what I knew was sure to come, my breathing slowed as our kisses became unanimous. Circling her fingers around my clitoris sent shock waves radiating throughout my body. Throbbing uncontrollably, my pussy continued to pulsate with each warranted touch.

As she bent down and began nibbling around the rim of my panties, the vision was more than I could bear. The picture and inherent feeling began to take over my emotions. Forcibly pulling my panties to the side, Karen softly began kissing my inner thighs as she gradually made her way to the lips of my pussy. In that very moment, life for me seemed to come to an abrupt halt.

 I couldn't decipher if it was the forbidden fact that I was with another woman, or the actual feeling that she was giving me. All I knew for now was that the feeling was unexplainable. Deeply breathing in the night air, I began panting, as I could no longer control my emotions.

Sucking gently on the top of my pussy, she slowly slid her tongue down the crevasse of my vagina before sliding it directly inside of me. Gliding back and forth, she flickered her tongue within the walls of my vagina rapidly, as if it was a pick on a set of guitar strings.

Feeling the unmistakable feelings of an oncoming orgasm, my concentration was suddenly broken with the sound of the glass door slowly opening. Stepping out with a crude yet pleased look on his face was Merlich.

"My, my, my, so this is where the party is happening," said Merlich as he stood at the edge of the door, continuing to smile.

Startled, I jerked backwards as his emergence took me by surprise. Carrying on as if nothing was happening, Karen continued to lick and suck on me as if I were a warm tasty treat. Although caught up in the moment, I couldn't help but ponder on whether this was actually her first encounter. She seemed too experienced and too matter of fact about the entire situation.

"Is it my turn yet?" asked Merlich as he emerged from the doorway.

Still startled but unable to speak, I closed my eyes as I moaned and groaned, consciously making efforts to invigorate the feelings that had brought on the previous interrupted orgasm. No longer alarmed by his presence, I began squirming in the chair when I suddenly felt an extra set of hands rest squarely on my thigh.

Opening my eyes briefly, I took pleasure in seeing Merlich and Karen as they each ran both of their tongues up and down the walls of my pussy. The vision itself was like no other. I felt superior and domineering, like a queen on her throne enjoying the treatment of her peasants. I became exhilarated by the vision and feeling, as the undeniable sounds of moaning and smacking emitted through the dark night sky. Tonguing each other in between, the two continued on until I felt depleted and practically sucked dry.

Finally standing up, Merlich unzipped his pants and pulled out a hardened, vein-popping dick; he stood over Karen and I as he stroked it back and forth. As if it were a practice-taught command, Karen immediately centered herself in a squatting position, veering her head towards Merlich as she rubbed me with one hand while using the other hand to stroke him. Shifting back and forth between his dick and my pussy, Karen's methodical rhythmic motions would make the most seasoned porn star look like a rookie starring in a home video; this bitch had skills. The visual and feelings it brought on became intoxicating, as my body began to tense up with the compulsory feeling of another orgasm beginning to make its way.

Grabbing her by the front of her throat, Merlich slowly raised her up to a standing position.

"Take off just the bottom piece," he ordered.

Slipping out of her panties, Karen immediately did as she was told. Once again grabbing her by the neck, he slung her body onto the rails of the balcony before coming up behind her. Now holding her by the back of her neck, he crouched down slightly as he seemed to embed himself inside of her. Pumping back and forth vigorously, he let go of her neck as he quickly grabbed the back of her hair, twining it within his fingers as if to secure his grip before reverting back to his fanatical pumping motions.

The sounds of Karen shrieking louder and louder seemed to intensify his force. Looking over at me while I sat in the chair now masturbating, his movements became even more fanatical as he visually began shaking with accompanying shallow breaths.

"Get on your knees, I'm about to cum," said Merlich through aspirated breaths.

As instructed, Karen dropped to her knees as Merlich stood over her feverishly pumping his dick. Within seconds, a long white stream of cum shot right over Karen's eye, as the remainder slowly dripped down onto her face.

∞∞∞

The rest of the week in New York was nothing short of memorable. After each daily conference, Karen and I would attend shows, go out shopping, or simply just lounge around at the hotel; all at the expense of Merlich of course.

After everything that had been said and done with Karen and Merlich, I was certain that things would be awkward and I would probably have to find a room on the other side of town. But to my surprise, the festivities of the first night were never again brought up. It was as if it never happened—and for me that was surety enough.

To be quite honest, I don't think I can ever look at any of them quite the same again. Merlich was my boss and Karen was my best friend. Together we had crossed into untrodden territory that, even in my wildest dreams, I couldn't have imagined. Though pleasing at the time, I can't help but wonder if things will remain the same once we got back to Miami—or will there be some kind of adverse aftermath? It was puzzling to consider, but for now, I guess I'll just take everything one day at a time.

As the week drew to a close, I became more and more excited as I eagerly anticipated my meeting with Chanlor. In less than eight hours I would be lying in the arms of my king, and possibly lounging at an elegant French reserve. As I sat on the plane reflecting on my life, my eyes began to get heavy the very moment the flight attendants began their safety protocol speech.

After what felt like an hour or so sleep, my neck suddenly jerked as the pain of trying to sleep upright took its apparent toll. Moving around in stretching motions, the intercom flickered before the voice of the captain was heard, instructing the flight attendants to prepare for arrival.

Looking out the window in shock, I could see stretches of land in the distance, which confirmed that arrival was in fact near. I couldn't believe that I had slept over seven hours in an uncomfortable upright position. I guess the activities of the week took a toll on my already stressed body.

Pulling out my make-up bag, I checked out my face in my compact mirror before applying powder, blusher, and a little Candy Yum Yum lipstick. Running my fingers through my hair, I pulled on my curls to make sure that everything was laid to perfection. The moment the plane's wheels hit the graveled runway ironically gave me a feeling of pins and needles. A natural at meeting and landing promising men, my sudden jitteriness came as a shock. It was just something about him, something that I have inherently yearned for quite some time now.

Gathering my things, I headed out of the plane and into Heathrow International Airport. To no surprise, the place was buzzing with people from every corner of the world. With it being my first trip to the UK, I anxiously looked out the windows to observe the outdoor scenery. Seeing much of the same as any other airport, I continued along to the baggage claim, where Chanlor's driver would be waiting.

"Long flight, huh?" said a nicely dressed woman standing beside me at the baggage terminal.

"Very. I managed to sleep most of it away, though," I replied to the lady, smiling slightly.

"Lucky for you, the seats were just too uncomfortable for me to get any shut eye."

"They really are, but I had a really long week in New York, so I didn't have to really try."

"Yeah, I did as well. I work for JP Morgan and we had to attend a conference there this week. So since I had a little vacation time left, I figured I would just go visit family."

"Really? I was there on business as well," I replied before continuing, "Was it the high yield bond conference?"

"Why, yes, it was. Were you there?" she asked.

"What do you know, small world. Myself and a couple other co-workers flew up for the week to attend it. By the way, I'm Leah. Leah Miller," I added as I extended my hand for a shake.

"Well, nice to meet you, Leah, I'm Rebecca Haimowitz."

As we continued talking, she went on to say that she would be staying in London for the next month to not only visit family, but to carry out a few new business deals. Her family apparently owned a lot of businesses in the metro area, and she and her brother were the ones mostly in charge of them. Intrigued by her business savvy, I suggested that we exchange numbers and possibly meet up for lunch sometime during my stay. Happily in agreement, we exchanged numbers before parting ways. Being that my phone was almost dead, I decided to write her number down on a piece of paper and toss it in the pocket of my purse.

As I made my way down the escalators, I could see several men in suits holding signs with different names on them. Getting further down, my eyes bopped from sign to sign in search of my name.

Within seconds I could vividly see an older man holding a sign that read *Lee-Lee*. Certain that it was a cute gesture from Chanlor, I smiled as I made my way over to him.

"Excuse me, but is Lee-Lee possibly short for Leah?" I asked.

"Leah Miller?" he inserted with a deep British accent and smile.

"That'll be me," I happily responded.

"Wonderful, the name is Alex and it is a pleasure to meet you."

"Nice to meet you as well, Alex," I responded with a smile.

"Right this way. Mr. C is anxiously awaiting your arrival," replied the driver as he ushered me to the waiting vehicle.

The moment I stepped outside of the building, I was immediately hit in the face with unusually cool and gloomy weather—as if rain was in the distance. Although sunshine on the first day would have been great, the rain would most likely force Chanlor and I to remain inside; at least for the rest of the night.

"Madame," said the driver as he opened the door of silver BMW.

Climbing inside, I was greeted with a bottle of wine and a glass that sat squarely on one end of the seat.

"A bottle of wine was requested by Mr. C for your drinking pleasure, as the airport is quite a bit of distance from the manor," added Alex as he got in the car and adjusted the rearview mirror.

"How nice of him," I replied as I lifted the cork out of the wine bottle.

After pouring myself a glass, I placed the remainder of the wine in the chiller as I sat back to enjoy the ride.

Don't worry, I'm on my way baby, I mumbled internally. *Just make sure that you're ready for me.*

« CHAPTER 19 »

As I TRIED TO MOVE AROUND, I somehow felt restricted, as if something was holding my wrist. Struggling to open my eyes, I was continually greeted with absolute darkness each and every time. Unsure of what to make of my encounter, I closed my eyes again before quickly reopening them. Faced with much of the same, I lunged my body in an upward position, only to be forced back down by some form of a metal restraint. Still unable to see, I attempted to stretch my fingers near my wrist, but was unsuccessful as my body quickly flopped back down. Wiggling my wrist in the metal holding that seemed to have tightening grooves, confirmed that it was in fact a metal pair of handcuffs.

The inability to see or move while being chained with handcuffs caused my breathing to increase and mind to race. Feeling like an animal trapped in a cage, I let out a gut-wrenching scream as I pulled and tugged at the handcuffs before hearing the sound of the door slowly screech open.

"Quiet down," said the voice in the distance.

"Hello? Please help me! Where am I and why am I in handcuffs? This has to be some kind of mistake," I quickly asked, moving my head around in fear.

"Someone will be in to speak to you. Until then, I need you to remain quiet or you will without hesitation be punished," said the deep cold voice.

As I heard the tapping of his shoes and the sounds of the door apparently screeching to a close, I immediately yelled, "Please wait! Where am I? My name is Leah and I am an American; I'm supposed to be here with Mr. Chanlor...."

And then it hit me. I didn't even know Chanlor's last name. I was so caught up in the money that I was receiving that I never took the time to even ask the most basic of details; details that without a doubt could possibly save me from this horrendous case of apparent mistaken identity.

"Shut up!" yelled the mysterious guy before continuing. "As I said, if you don't remain quiet, I will make sure to silence you.

Afraid to continue on, I decided to remain quiet as I continued lying on what felt like a springy old mattress-- while in despair I made attempts to wrap my head around what was going on.

"Okay, Leah, calm down. You're in another country and obviously something went wrong and you ended up in the wrong place; that's all. When the next person comes in, just explain to them who you are and everything will be okay; Chanlor will take care of it," I continued repeating to myself in an attempt to stay at ease.

Overwhelmed with fear and uncertainty, I could no longer control my emotions as I uncontrollably let out a bloodcurdling scream, desperate for anyone to hear my torturous cries.

As I continued to scream, the familiar sound of the screeching door radiated throughout the room yet again.

"Hello, who's there?" I asked, flashing my head around blindly in fear of what may come from my screams.

"Leah!"

The sound of the familiar voice turned my fears into sheer happiness.

"Chanlor, oh thank God—baby, please help me, take these God awful chains off me. Where am I?"

As I sat on the bed awaiting his touch and help, a gawky eerie silence filled the air.

"Chanlor? Are you still there?"

"Leah, Leah, Leah," said Chanlor as the sounds of his tapping footsteps echoed throughout the room. "I really hate to be the one to tell you this, but you are in the right place, my dear."

"No, no this must be a mistake. Baby, it's me, Leah, we've been—"

"Silence!" shouted Chanlor in an unusual angry tone. "From now on, you will ask to speak before you do so. I've had enough of your constant chatter and fucking disrespect. Now, let me explain what will happen here. You are now considered my property. You must at all times do as you are instructed or there will be dire consequences to pay. I have a very tight schedule that I adhere to and I expect you to abide by it willingly; even though unwillingly may be a little more exciting," he continued with an evil chuckle.

"I also need you to understand that this is a business and I intend on running it as such. Everything that you undergo is simply just that; business. Meals are served twice a day and will be brought to your room; that is if you have good behavior. I cannot stress enough that your full cooperation determines your overall treatment here. Therefore, I suggest that you follow all verbal commands, especially those of the head master," said Chanlor before continuing. "Now, you were saying?"

Paralyzed with fear, I tried gravely to make sense of everything that was happening. This either had to be another sick joke or a simple case of mistaken identity.

"Baby, I don't understand; it's me Leah. We met at the bowling alley in Miami and have practically been inseparable ever since. You bought my plane ticket from New York; we talked endlessly about how special our time would be once I got here. I don't understand...."

Just like before, he let out another evil laugh.

"My dear, of course I remember meeting you, but I will have you know that it wasn't me that you were talking to on the phone, but my young nephew who's in secondary school; who sounds very similar to me from what I hear. You don't really think that I have that sort of time on my hands, now do you?"

Speechless, I remained silent; I didn't know what to think, let alone say.

"You see, I am a very busy man and I run several successful businesses—as you know, and that part to be true." He continued with a slight chuckle. "But anyway, that is part of the reason why you're here. Your nosiness and prying ended up costing me a great deal of money; a very significant amount of money, actually."

"Chanlor, I'm terribly sorry. If it is the money that you sent to me, it's not a problem. I promise to pay it back, I never—"

"Shut your God damn mouth, woman! Your mouth is your biggest enemy, you fucking harlot!" he shouted sternly and angrily. "That is exactly why you're in this position! Now, as I was saying, you cost me a great deal of money, and now you must pay it back by no other means than your services. You are contracted to be my sex slave for a period of approximately two years. More if I so please. Once you are released, all information about myself and my establishment must remain a secret. If any, and I mean the smallest amount of information is leaked, whether here or the States, you will be immediately tracked down and silenced," added Chanlor before continuing. "In case you think this is a joke, your family lives off Summer Drive, and you have a nice looking sister that I wouldn't mind having as well. So, not only do I expect your full cooperation but your family does as well."

"You bastard, you better not touch my fucking sister," I yelled as I pulled angrily at the handcuffs.

SPLAT....

I screamed out in pain as the sting of his slap lingered on my face.

"There will be more of that if you don't shut your filthy little mouth," said Chanlor through what sounded like clinched teeth. "I don't how Charles put up with you!"

The sound of the forbidden name caused my heart to drop to my knees as my palms began to sweat.

"Oh yes, you heard it right. Leah, Charles was one of my best workers and a very good friend of mine as well. We had several successful deals going on until you put your stinky little nose in the operation, bringing in that pig of a detective friend of yours. Now my Florida operation is pretty much in sands and most of my bishops and knights there have no direction," he continued.

"Even Steven, one of my strongest soldiers who has recruited a great deal of women for me, has gone AWOL. The bastard fell in love with the last woman that he was to send over— as he did you!"

"Thanks to one of my new rooks, Justin, she was quickly swept up, brought here, and put to work—which is exactly how I found you. With the help of your sister, I knew everything that I needed to know about you. I must admit that at that time I immediately knew I had something special on my hands. Something to make me the money that I had lost and men would be willing to pay top dollar for. The more information that I got on you, the more I knew I needed to have you. There was no way I was letting that weak, poor excuse of a businessman Steven get in the way.

"But I must say that there is a light at the end of the tunnel, my dear; believe it or not, out of all of this there is in fact good news. Instead of being a low class slave and having to sleep with whoever pays, I may want to keep you for myself. My own personal playmate, if you will. Rather exciting, wouldn't you agree; after all I am your secret admirer.

Unsure whether to answer or not, I knew without a doubt that this time I had really fucked up. I was in far above my head. I had ventured into dangerous territory that ran deeper than I could ever have imagined. But, like the strong person I've always been known to be, I wasn't about to lie down without a fight.

I will surrender to your little game for now, Mr. Chanlor, but trust and believe, hell has no fury like a woman scorned.

About the author

Kaydeen A. Hutchinson, native of Jamaica, is an author, journalist, and overall professional. She holds an MBA with a concentration in Public Administration and a Bachelor of Science in Applied Management. She currently resides in Southern Florida with her five year old son TJ, and enjoys socializing, reading, writing, and traveling.

Kaydeen would love to hear your thoughts. Please feel free to visit her or email her at:

Kaydeen@kaydeenahutchinson.com

Kaydeenahutchinson.com